DEATH in
Titipu

Barbara Yates Rothwell

Order this book online at www.trafford.com
or email orders@trafford.com

Most Trafford titles are also available at major online book retailers.

Print information available on the last page.

ISBN: 978-1-4907-7765-8 (sc)
ISBN: 978-1-4907-7767-2 (hc)
ISBN: 978-1-4907-7766-5 (e)

Trafford rev.   10/06/2016

www.trafford.com
North America & international
toll-free: 1 888 232 4444 (USA & Canada)
fax: 812 355 4082

Murder is never funny, but I think most people concerned with solving such a crime would agree that some of the folks involved have their peculiar side. A few of them are in here.

This tale takes us back to the days when police had to manage without many of today's electronic aids to assist them, and with what might seem now to be archaic forensic methods. Enjoy!

'I was always thought, as a young person, to have a rather fine voice,' Miss Teresa Glencosset was saying in the well-rounded tones familiar to her students. 'There was talk of my undertaking a singing career. But it was considered by my parents to be a hazardous future for a young woman, and common-sense prevailed.'

She directed her wolfish smile swiftly around the company assembled in the Green Room. 'So my little annual foray into G and S is for me a small acknowledgement of "what might have been".'

'What would you have sung if you had turned pro?' someone asked. Miss Glencosset raised thoughtful eyebrows and regarded a poster of last year's *Pirates* absently.

'Opera, I think. I always felt I had the *presence* for it.'

'Makes a bloody formidable Katisha, anyway,' Stephen Harcourt muttered to his neighbour. 'I blench every time she advances on me. Never know whether she's going to embrace me or swallow me.'

Jasper Spenlow stretched his arms above his head and yawned. A general sense of movement replaced the inertia that had itself replaced an outpouring of energy on stage throughout the evening. After a week of rehearsals, Jasper felt that musically, at least, *Mikado* was progressing according to schedule. Little Dulcet Merridew collected the coffee cups (that was Dulcet for you, always the willing slave), and carted them off to the tiny kitchen; Jasper's wife, Maggie, picked up scripts and vocal scores and strode out again on to the stage to make sure that nothing of value had been left.

He watched her; no amount of activity, no rehearsal traumas, ever seemed to recue that nervous energy to the level at which most people existed. She would be that way until bedtime; and then, as her head hit the pillow, she would be off into sleep, storing up more energy for what the morrow might bring. He envied her.

The Reverend Charles Culbert, vicar of this parish of St Edmund, gave out a sigh and rose from the depths of the one comfortable chair. With his long, angular legs and a perpetually solemn expression, he was rather too like a praying mantis to be taken seriously out of his usual milieu. In the pulpit he had a certain distant charm, as if by being physically lifted above the common people in the pews below he had somehow achieved a sort of spiritual loftiness; why he found the annual romp of the Gilbert and Sullivan production so attractive, Jasper had never understood. On the face of it he was no actor. But something clicked once the costume and the grease paint were on; then the Rev Mr Culbert came to life, and there was something about the sight of their vicar representing the morally devious Pooh-Bah that gave the groundlings particular pleasure.

Culbert looked across the room to where Molly de Vance was discussing costumes with Mary Harcourt, whose nimble fingers came into their own at performance time. Molly was standing with her back towards him, and after a moment he turned, nodded to Jasper and the others who were preparing to leave, and went out into the night.

He walked slowly towards the rectory, which would be clammy and unwelcoming because he had forgotten to build up the wood stove, and because there would be no one there to greet him. It was a matter of astonishment to him that after a lifetime spent in almost monastic seclusion (of his own choice, for he was basically a solitary man) he should recently have developed a strange craving for human company.

The evening was pleasantly cool; but it is likely that he would not have noticed had icicles hung by the wall. For the Rev Charles was prey to emotions until now unknown to him. There had been (he recalled this dimly as down a long corridor of time) a young lady, earnestly bespectacled, for whom he had felt affection during his final university year. They had drunk coffee together, walked a couple of times across the campus, and then—why, he could not now remember—lost touch with each other. But that gently warm, wholly chaste relationship had nothing to do with the extraordinary and highly alarming sensations now consuming him in a most improper manner.

'O my dove, that art in the clefts of the rock, in the secret places of the stars, let me see thy countenance, let me hear thy voice...' he yearned. But the night was silent, give or take a strident red wattle bird or two, and the roar of Dave Shafto's motor bike as it sped away from the theatre.

Young Shafto's mind, like all Gaul, was divided three ways. In one compartment were the pages and pages required to be learnt before he could claim to have the role of Nanki-Poo under his belt; in another he maintained a kind of human computer that listened to the volume of sound coming from his vehicle and analysed it, piston-stroke by piston-stroke; and in the third was a dark cloud of foreboding that he tried hard to ignore, but which was coming closer, growing ever more threatening, reducing him to frightened, shaming apprehension.

In defiance, shaking a metaphorical finger at fate, he revved the engine and shot through the sleepy town at full speed, avoiding a confrontation with the police by seconds.

Simon Lee, product of an English mother and Chinese father, locked the theatre door and shook it to make sure. As president of the society this year he took his duties very seriously. He opened his car door, singing in a pleasant baritone voice *'Three little girls from school are we...'* It struck him as quite odd that this mock-Japanese comedy, relating back to a time when the Japanese were simply people who lived a long way away and wore funny clothes, should still be popular in a society that had seen its fill of the horrors of a militaristic regime storming down through the islands of the Pacific.

He switched to *'to make the punishment fit the crime...'* and remembered, briefly, his father, whose contact with the Japanese had involved punishment where no crime had been committed. Mr Lee senior had died of it.

Stephen and Mary Harcourt walked home. It was only five minutes, door to door, and it had been a long and busy day. Mary did complicated calculations in her head, five metres of this, ten of that, and a good length of something for the sashes—'obis' they called them. Mary did crossword puzzles, so she knew the word well. 'Light blue on purple looks rather nice,' she said, but Stephen didn't answer.

He was engrossed in his own thoughts. This was a bad time for 'Mikado' and his business interests to collide. He enjoyed the part of Koko (saw something of his own duplicity in it, if he was honest), but with this big property development just coming to the boil it was a nuisance to have to give a part of his mind to the frivolity of a Savoy Opera. *'Tit-willow,'* he hummed; *'tit-willow... tit-willow!'*

'The girls are good,' Mary said as they pushed open the garden gate. She meant the school-girl trio. 'Pattie's a natural, don't you think?'

He grunted. 'Not so keen on the Percy girl. Sings sharp.'

'That's just nerves. She'll do well. And Corinne...'

'Pretty girl! Sympathetic. Should go far.' He based his knowledge of her on a brief encounter backstage during last year's *Pirates* when she had taken seriously the blackened nail—gained through a too hearty effort with the scenery—which Mary had failed to coo over.

As they closed the door behind them an ancient utility clattered past, loaded beyond good sense with the bower bird collection of bits and pieces that would go to make a successful show. 'Bingo' Rafferty, props man extraordinaire, had a Midas touch with junk, transmuting it into sets, furnishings and all the paraphernalia of theatricality. His weatherboard house, on the edge of town, was one of the local sights, almost lost beneath piles of this and heaps of that, an eyesore or an Ali Baba's cave according to one's standards.

A mile further on, where the landscape had been sculpted into conformity but was close enough to the raw bush to warrant the description of 'countryside', Miss Glencosset locked her garage door and made her way into the dark confines of the headmistress's house. Behind it stood the solid block that was St Chedwyn's School for Girls. In its dormitories lay seventy-five young ladies about to be unleashed on to the world; and in the morning another one hundred would be bussed in for the day's dose of learning.

St Chedwyn's was Miss Glencosset's glory, her *raison d'être*, the emergence from a life spent in doing the will of others; sometimes, when there was no one looking, she patted the dark-brick walls to let them know how deeply she cared, how much they meant to her.

With Stephen Harcourt as Chairman of the Governors, Jasper Spenlow dividing his time as Director of Music between St C's and the state high school in the next town, and a staff bending to her every whim, she felt a sense of security, of power, of educational rightness, that carried her up to her bedroom in a cloud of euphoric pleasure.

Molly de Vance tied a gaily-coloured scarf over her red curls and waved crimson finger-nails towards Michael Kowalski, whose attempts to get her into his butcher's van for the short trip home had once again been neatly foiled. He stared after her with frustrated longing, his broad face hiding nothing of his feelings.

'Silly thing!' Molly thought as she clipped her way across the road. 'Do I *look* like a butcher's wife? Honestly!' She recalled for a fractional moment the other eyes that had regarded her across the room, and grinned to herself. She'd had a bit of fun teasing the poor old thing—but she certainly didn't see herself as a *vicar's* wife! Come to that, she wasn't that keen on the word 'wife', anyway. It had a narrow, constricting sound to it. Not like 'mistress', 'courtesan', even 'de facto'. Though from what she'd seen of her friends, 'de facto' wasn't much cop, either. It was still a man's world. Not easy for a woman to take her fun on the run, even in these permissive days. Not in this poky little town, at least. She wondered if it would be more to her liking in Sydney. Perhaps she should travel again...

She reached her driveway and was aware that the butcher's van had taken a sudden turn of speed and shot past her. She grinned again, secretly. Silly twit! Couldn't take no for an answer.

2

Bella Parkinson measured a neat distance from the edge of the window and carefully placed a handbill where it would be seen, using precise little pieces of sticky tape to secure it. Then she stepped outside the shop to check that it was properly aligned. That was Bella. She liked things to be just so.

Above her the newly painted shop front announced '*Chester Parkinson, Pharmacist*'. It gave Bella much innocent pleasure to see it. It was a name with dignity; and Chester lived up to it. No one would ever call him 'Ches'—he was the sort of man who commanded respect, and this meant a great deal to her. She felt that if he had given her nothing else, he had bestowed a kind of status upon her; and she managed to be grateful for it. A mischievous imp whispered in her ear as she went to the back of the shop that she would have preferred a couple of children—or even a dog, a small one that she could cuddle on her knee. But she silenced the imp with a shake of her head. That was all behind them now. It was partly her fault, anyway. They should have talked it over before they married.

'Mrs Lambert's pills are ready,' Chester said, slapping a label on the packet. 'And we're nearly out of that new line of soap.'

'I'll put it on the order, Chester.'

It seemed to her sometimes that they were playing a game together, as if one day Chester had said, 'I know, let's pretend I'm a chemist, and we'll have a shop and you can be my assistant and we'll wear white coats and dole out pills and cough medicine and everyone will respect us.' And she had said, 'Oh, yes, Chester—let's!'

And so they had done, for nearly twenty years; and sometimes she wished that they could play something else for a change—fish and chips, or ladies' knitwear, or fruit and vegies. But that was silly, because Chester had qualified as a pharmacist all those years ago, and if you were a highly respected qualified pharmacist that was what you did.

So she enjoyed these few weeks in the year when she *could* forget who she was, just for a while, learning words and music and steps in Jasper Spenlow's chorus. Last year she had been in *'Pirates'*, the year before in *'Yeomen'*; and Chester, not aspiring to the stage but believing in marital solidarity, undertook the role of treasurer to the society, and often sat in the darkened back of the theatre while Bella pretended she was somebody else.

This year it was more exciting than usual, for during the auditions Jasper had regarded her with a calculating eye and then suggested she should understudy for Katisha. 'You've got the quality of voice,' he said, 'though too small. Can you sing louder? Well, anyway…' and she had gone home in a state of twitter that had taken all her acting ability to hide from her husband.

'Good auditions?' he had asked without looking up; and she had nodded and taken off her scarf and subdued her inner exuberance.

'Very good, thank you, dear. Jasper was very pleased.' She hesitated only briefly. 'As a matter of fact he's asked me to be one of the understudies—for Katisha.'

Chester had glanced up over his glasses. 'Katisha? Good lord! You? You're nothing like Katisha!'

'He says I have the quality of voice. Though small.'

'Well, I must say I don't agree with him. I always see Katisha as a bit strident—a bit on the coarse side. Surely he must have someone more—more…'

'Well,' Bella said, not disappointed, because Chester had such high standards and would offer opinions, as he often said, without fear or favour, 'he seemed to think…'

'Anyway,' her husband said, going back to the shop accounts spread before him on the table, 'Miss Glencosset is never ill, so they won't have to call on you.'

Bella went through to the bedroom and stood before the mirror, examining herself with a critical eye. Now that she thought about it, the idea was clearly ridiculous. She didn't have what Miss Glencosset called 'the presence'; her face was placidly middle-aged—though perhaps with make-up…? And above all, she was not a dominating person. Which both Miss Glencosset *and* Katisha indisputably were.

With some fervour she wished Teresa Glencosset well for the run of the operetta.

Miss Glencosset was indeed in excellent health. Perhaps a little overweight these days—headmistressing tended to be more sedentary than classroom teaching had been—but she kept to a strict regimen and included a game of tennis in her busy day whenever the opportunity presented itself.

The secret of success, she had found, was to have a programme and *stick to it!* This was what she always told her girls. Each day was carefully planned the previous evening, and in this way she was able to include not only the essential activities posed by her job, but also such personal pleasures as her annual involvement with Gilbert and Sullivan. The desk diary pages were gradually engulfed as the year moved on by precise lines of detail, the skeleton or blue-print or what-have-you upon which her life depended.

Running parallel with this framework were the other diaries, in which more personal matters were immortalised. They were splendid leather-bound books, fleshing out the bones of the daily round; her raw material, she hoped, for the autobiographical work she intended to write in her retirement.

Tonight, after rehearsal, she sat at her desk under the gentle light of the electrified oil lamp and planned the day to come, pinning it down with times and places as precisely as a butterfly captured in a showcase.

'3.30 pm: visit of Prof Ed Pultry, to discuss development of studies in biology.

4.15 pm: tea in study with Prof E.P.

4.45 pm: Prof E.P. leaving. See Matron about Muriel Smith's impetigo.'

Once the day ahead had been netted and secured, she turned to the current leather-bound repository of her more evanescent thoughts and feelings.

'*Excellent rehearsal. J Spenlow meticulous as always. A fine music director, in spite of everything, bearing out the promise of earlier years!! His wife's overall direction imaginative and inspiring. But sense that all is not...*' (she stopped, searching for words), '*is not as they would have us think.*' (A bit vague there; she would be more precise when she knew better what the situation really was).

'*J S has chosen Bella Parkinson as my understudy! An odd choice by any standards. BP overshadowed by husband. One wonders why women allow themselves to be eaten alive by the most extraordinarily boring little men. Ah well! Must see to it that I do not fall by the wayside. Cannot imagine Mrs P putting the fear of God into Koko.*'

She wrote steadily for a few more minutes and then, the day at last suitably completed, made a cup of cocoa and sat down for a while with the score of 'Mikado', refreshing her memory and savouring the pleasure she found in slipping into the character of the fearsome Katisha. As she was climbing into bed she had a sudden thought; a thin and malicious smile crossed her face. 'What a fool the Culbert man is!' She pulled up the blankets. 'Casting sheep's eyes at that dreadful Molly. Surely he would have more sense than to become involved with such a silly little tart—at his age, and a man of the cloth too!'

She adjusted the electric blanket and stretched her toes to the bottom of the bedclothes. The vicar had been quite odd this evening. Odder than usual, that is. She always found him very unsatisfactory, as man and a cleric; though his Pooh-Bah was quite reasonably effective, it had to be admitted. Well, she promised herself, she would keep her eyes open; all was grist to her mill. 'Do they still unfrock them?' she murmured aloud, sliding away into the arms of Morpheus (a phrase she had always found particularly poetic).

Maggie Spenlow was never entirely satisfied—it was her nature to be critical. If all the principals were doing well you could look for problems with the chorus; if the scenery was up to schedule there would inevitably be a disaster in the costume department. That was the essence of the theatre—certainly the amateur theatre, where unbelievable hazards awaited the unwary.

But it had been a good rehearsal, by and large. She took the cup of coffee Jasper offered her and put up her feet.

'Pleased?' Jasper said, a mite nervously.

Maggie shrugged. 'We might get on better if Nanki-Poo could keep his mind on the job. And what the vicar thinks he's doing ogling Molly like that I can't quite imagine. Doesn't he *know* her reputation? I wish they wouldn't bring their personal lives on stage.'

'They're not as skilled in dissembling as we are.'

'What *do* you mean?' She shot a cold glance at him. 'Dissembling?'

'I mean that no one could suspect that we are not a devoted couple.'

'What's "devoted"?' she said scornfully. 'We work well together, don't we? We get results. We respect each other's achievements. What more do you want?'

'*Ah,*' Jasper thought, sinking down into the couch and watching the coffee in his cup as he swirled it round absently, '*what indeed? A little of what the outrageous Molly is reputed to offer? The devotion of Bella Parkinson for her stolid husband? The curvy promise of Pattie Fisher, adorable Yum-Yum to Dave Shafto's spotty Nanki-Poo*' Why had he so often gone for dominating women, frequently against his own better judgement, when what he had really wanted was a comfy, sexy little creature who would make him feel tall and manly and exciting?

Maggie caught his eye and he smiled hopefully. But his wife, after a quelling moment, turned away. 'I think we do perfectly well as we are,' she said, closing the subject.

In his bed, in the room which had once been for visitors and was now his 'den', Jasper tried to convince himself that she was right.

3

Stephen Harcourt, was 'not available', 'in a meeting', whatever was the current put-off for callers. Sylvia Milton enjoyed the sensations of reflected power when she skilfully diverted them, and warmed herself in Mr Harcourt's approval. She had been with his company for over ten years, and in a kind of blissful innocence regarded herself as his (dared she even think it?) 'corporate spouse'. In no way did she wish to usurp Mrs Harcourt's place; under no circumstances would she ever have thought of her boss in sexual terms. But she felt a link, a strong relationship with him, which was so precious that if the thought of retirement—his or hers—ever crossed her mind she felt a cold shiver through her heart.

So when the phone rang and an angry voice attacked her through the receiver (and this had happened a number of times lately) Sylvia took satisfaction in saying, her own voice sweet as honey, that 'Mr Harcourt is in a meeting. No, he cannot be reached at this time. Please leave your number and I will see that he gets back to you.'

'You've said that the last three times, sweetheart!' the voice said, insultingly, and Sylvia bristled. 'Tell Harcourt that he gets back to me—or else!'

'Or else what?' she asked coolly. 'Are you threatening Mr Harcourt?'

'You bet your sweet life I'm threatening him, kiddo!' The phone was cut off abruptly. Sylvia stood for a moment before replacing her own receiver gently. Through the glass partition she could see Stephen Harcourt at his desk, unrolling the top one of a pile of draughtsman's plans. He had taken his jacket off, and the sight of him brought out all her frustrated maternal instincts. 'They shall not pass!' she told herself dramatically, feeling that she was probably quoting something heroic. Whatever might threaten him, she would temper the wind, turn back the hordes, stand, if necessary, at the door with arms spread in defiance. It did not occur to her to wonder why the caller should be so angry.

'Mikado' proceeded according to expectation, which is to say that there were days when everyone wished the season could be cancelled, and others when excitement became intense and a sense of euphoria filled the small theatre.

In the fortnight before the dress rehearsal the tensions began to rise, with personalities sharpening like drawn swords and things said which had been better left unsaid. Maggie Spenlow, sitting at the back of the stalls—several seats away from Chester Parkinson, to avoid having to talk—watched the stresses unconcerned. It was a good way of generating emotions, of breaking free from the social inhibitions: as long as it didn't go too far.

Chester, his mind far from the theatre, was watching a long procession of dollar signs crossing his mental vision, rather like the sheep one conjures up to woo sleep. But these were unwelcome. Each sign carried a little minus symbol before it, and the whole jigging, neurotic procedure was fiercely red. Behind the cavalcade, outlined in red ink, was the face of his bank manager. Chester tried to avoid seeing its expression, but he knew it was not one of tolerant understanding. In desperation he dragged his thoughts back to what was happening on stage.

'It is far too fast,' Teresa Glencosset was saying. *'Far* too fast. Helter-skelter! Words inaudible.' She demonstrated, gabbling. *'There is beauty in the bellow of the blast...'!* There, you see, Jasper. No time to draw breath. After all, this *is* one of my big moments.' She turned to Stephen Harcourt. 'Don't you agree, Koko?'

'Oh, certainly,' he said, though with the air of one who has lost his way in an argument. 'Oh—certainly...er...Katisha' He pulled himself together. 'Too fast, old man,' he said firmly, nodding first at Jasper and then at Miss Glencosset.

Jasper sighed. 'All right. Try it again.' He turned to the 'orchestra'—six basic instruments and a piano. 'A little less *prestissimo*—perhaps more of a *presto*. But it must be crisp. Crisp! Lively! No slithering about. Plenty of staccato, good clean dotted notes. OK? Right!' He lifted his baton. Teresa Glencosset lifted her chin. After a dozen bars he had to concede, annoyed, that she was right. It *had* been too fast.

Stephen Harcourt, ready to take up his role as Koko, Lord High Executioner, wished he could utilise his executioner's axe to cut his way through the morass of regulations and instructions he fought with every day. He was tired; when they got 'Mikado' over he'd have a break—take Mary away for a week's holiday somewhere warm, with the sea at the door and a row of shops to keep her happy. He liked to keep Mary happy; it made life a great deal easier at home.

Katisha had concluded her argument with Jasper, and the orchestra began once more to scrape its way into the introduction.

'Are you ready?' Miss Glencosset demanded with some asperity. 'Are you *ready*, Stephen?' Yes, he was ready; ready to drop.

The rehearsal ploughed on. The final scenes were a shambles. Jasper's head was in his hands as the last chords groaned their way into an uneasy silence. Maggie, coming down through the auditorium, was brusque.

'Go home, for God's sake! Learn your parts! Find out where you're supposed to stand. Try to stay on speaking terms until it's all over. Get a good night's sleep. And be back here, ready to go, on Friday night at seven. No later!' She looked up from the front of the stage at the eyes directed towards her. At the back she could see Mr Culbert, his face suitably penitent at the failures of himself and others. 'This is *Mikado*, damn it! Everyone knows it.' She gave a sudden sardonic grim. 'And—Vicar, pray for us!'

The meeting broke up in laughter. Miss Glencosset, quite at ease now that the rehearsal was over, smiled graciously as she passed the three little maids; Natalie, with an oddly secretive twist to her mouth, pretended not to see her. The Harcourts said good-night to the Parkinsons, and Kowalski, stepping out of his role as the Mikado, winked at Molly de Vance, a contact not missed by the Rev. Charles as he stood half concealed behind the curtains.

Culbert left by the stage door, nodding to Simon Lee, whose key was at the ready. Among the sounds of engines coming from the car park was the rich roar of Dave Shafto's motor-bike. Good-nights were being called, laughter exchanged. But in the vicar's heart was a splinter of ice. He knew that he was making an awful fool of himself over Molly—but somehow he no longer cared.

As he crossed the car-park he saw Miss Glencosset's car with its engine running, its parking lights on, and beside the driver's door a dark figure bending to the window.

'I probably know a great deal more than you think,' she was saying in her penetrating, jocular way. 'You'd be surprised!' And she laughed.

But the dark figure did not laugh; in the ill-lit car-park it was impossible to see who it was, though the low resonances of the answering voice suggested that it was a man. Culbert walked on without saying goodbye. He was too miserable to speak to anyone. Behind him he heard the headmistress's car rev and pull away; and before he had gained the adjacent road leading to the rectory the noises had all dissipated into the night, and he was quite alone.

Being alone was one thing, he was thinking wistfully; quite another to be so lonely.

By the evening before the dress rehearsal tempers were running high. Simon Lee, in his presidential role, watched with some apprehension as lifelong friendships threatened to shiver into fragments.

Molly de Vance had two or three of the men dancing attendance, but that was hardly unusual. Culbert, looking like a mournful rabbit, sat by himself to one side, only showing any life when he was Pooh-Bah. Kowalski, annoyed by Molly's infidelity, tried to get off with Natalie Percy and had his face slapped. And Dulcet Merridew, with Mary Harcourt and a small entourage of ladies armed with scissors and thimbles, sewing needles thrust into blouse fronts and lapels, grabbed anyone who was available for a final costume fitting.

Miss Glencosset, riding high above the *hoi poloi*, wore an expression of muted triumph; Lee wondered what she was up to.

The scene-building, which was going to need a miracle to be finished on schedule, was suddenly galvanised by the arrival of Bingo Rafferty.

'And about time!' Maggie exploded, hands on hips, glaring at him. 'Good of you to drop in!'

Bingo grinned, unconcerned. He knew Maggie of old. 'No sweat, Mags,' he said, hitching his jeans with one hand and hefting a hammer in the other. 'Have it done in half a tick. She's right!'

'Dress rehearsal tomorrow, Bingo. I don't think you realise...'

'Splash o' quick-dry paint on there,' he said cheerfully, pointing with the hammer. 'Coupla nails in there. An' I got a nice bit o' moulding'll go round the throne a treat, no worries! She's sweet, Mags. Coupla hours, maybe three.'

'Three days, more like. Bingo, you're a bloody menace!'

He grinned at her again, winking cheekily. 'An' you love me for it, Mags! Don't try to hide it.'

Maggie punched his shoulder with the nearest to affection she could muster. 'Don't let Jasper know, you evil man.' She looked around. 'Where *is* Jasper, anyway?'

'Talking to Miss Glencosset.' Pattie, with Dave Shafto in tow, was crossing the stage. She pointed behind her. Jasper was just emerging from the Green Room. Maggie regarded him thoughtfully before he saw her.

'He's looking quite old,' she thought, noticing the lines in the face, the drawn expression in the eyes. The idea surprised her. She herself felt so vibrant with energy that the concept of ageing repelled her. He should take more exercise, more vitamins. He had a duty to her to stay youthful—or at least to hold back the tides of middle-age. Maggie turned away irritably.

The day of the dress rehearsal opened with a torrential downpour and several claps of thunder. But then, as if the clerk of the weather had had second thoughts, the black clouds slid away and by mid-morning the skies were baby-blue with feathers of white clouds strategically placed around the horizon.

Within the theatre—an old converted cinema in the centre of town—sounds of hammering combined with Bingo's raucous baritone. Some way down the street, in the offices of Harcourt Developers, Sylvia Milton prepared to keep out the world so that Stephen could have peace and quiet before his big evening. When the phone rang she checked that it was not the anonymous insulter on the line before transferring it to her boss's waiting ear.

At St Chedwyn's, Miss Glencosset decided to make the most of the day she had kept free so that she would have abundant energy for the rehearsal. She played a set of tennis with an off-duty member of staff, strolled around the grounds, checking that the gardeners were not slacking off, then retired to her office. There she took out sundry of her leather-bound diaries and settled in a comfortable chair to browse. Idly she turned the pages—and smiled; it was high time some people faced up to their own stupidities. What a harvest festival of human weaknesses and futility! What a catch of empty-headed fish! Putting the phone where she could reach it easily, she lifted the receiver and dialled. In her eyes, as she waited for the connection, was a cold gleam of anticipation.

4

All things being equal (and how seldom they are in the theatre) the dress rehearsal was reasonably successful. Dulcet Merridew sat at the back of the auditorium, pinkly proud of her well-dressed show. On stage, Japanese ladies tripped gracefully, Japanese men strode masterfully; and, wonder of wonders, the scenery was excellent.

If some participants were more tense than others it was only to be expected. The chorus, finding security in numbers, enjoyed every moment; behind her fan, Molly gave bold invitations to at least half the men, with a wicked use of heavily disguised eyes.

Encased in costumes, anonymous in make-up, the Reverend Charles Culbert and Michael Kowalski the butcher gave of their best, helped considerably by the fact that they were never quite sure which one *was* Molly.

Three pretty girls teetered across stage, archly virginal; Natalie Percy managed not to sing sharp; in the French sense, Katisha was *formidable*, more than a match for Koko, who was pale, anxious—and sometimes even quite funny. And when it was over, the last note played, there was a moment's silence as everyone realised *they had done it!*

Then, from the dark auditorium, came the spatter of applause which was Maggie's and Jasper's and Dulcet's and Simon Lee's way of saying 'well done!' And the piercing whistle that was Bingo Rafferty's.

Someone had brought in a couple of bottles of something tasty; someone else had a carton of beer. The Green Room was alive with chatter and relieved laughter. In the two dressing rooms grease-paint-stained tissues littered the floor, and Dulcet and her little army pounced on costumes and hung them up ready for The Night. Slowly, noisily, in ones and twos, the cast left for home.

'You were splendid, dear,' Chester Parkinson said to Bella, who (because of her height) had been in the back row of the chorus.

'You could hardly have seen me,' she said, and was surprised when he took her arm and held her close.

'I can always see you,' he murmured, a little emotionally, she thought; she turned and gave him a kiss on the cheek.

'Dear Chester,' she said fondly. The vicar, passing them, wished them good-night in a pale, thin voice.

'You were so good,' Bella said to him. '*Such* a good performance.'

'How kind of you.' He sounded surprised rather than flattered, and slid away from them into the darkness.

'What a strange man,' she said in a low voice. 'Quite a paradox.'

The dust and excitement settled. Natalie, passing the dressing room door, was hailed from within. 'Help me off with this wretched wig,' Katisha called, emerging from under it a few moments later as a slightly dishevelled Miss Glencosset. 'Thank you, Natalie.'

She half-turned, looking over her shoulder at the girl. 'You did very well, my dear.'

Natalie kept her eyes down. 'Thanks, Miss Glencosset. You were pretty good yourself.'

'One has the experience!' For a moment their eyes met in the mirror. 'You must pop in again on Sunday afternoon and have a little chat, Natalie. I always find our little chats so interesting.'

Natalie hesitated for a moment, then nodded, lowering her gaze quickly. 'Yes, Miss Glencosset.'

As she left the room she could feel sharp eyes following her, and outside the door she shivered, once, before hurrying away into the dark.

At the mirror Teresa Glencosset concentrated on removing the thickly applied make-up, peering intently as her own strong complexion began to emerge from the Japanese white paint, absently singing a snatch of Katisha's song; and so she did not see a figure slide silently into the room, nor sense the hand raised above her with an oriental dagger, nor know anything more about her own sudden death than the blow to her back that made her gasp with shock, quite unable to cry out.

5

'You know something about music,' the Assistant Commissioner said. 'Did that festival case, didn't you? Pianists dying all over the place.'

Detective Sergeant Nicholas Henry Jarvis Verdun stared suspiciously at his superior. He was estimating the dangers of admitting that he had indeed mixed with the musical crowd during that trying time. 'That was me, sir, yes.'

'Got another one for you. Down in...' he perused the paper before him, 'down in the country somewhere. Schoolmistress been stabbed after a dress rehearsal for—oh, one of those Gilbert and Sullivan things. Where is it? Ah...' Yes, Mikado. That how you pronounce it? Mi-*kar*-do. Right? Well, get on down there and let's see what it's all about.' He handed the papers over. Nick took them and stood up.

'Who shall I take with me?'

'Young Briggs—OK? Lively lad, full of ideas.' He gazed just past Verdun's left ear, daring him to complain. Briggs was not noted for his efficient dedication.

'That'll do fine,' Verdun said, taking the wind out of his boss's sails. He turned towards the door, then looked back to the senior officer, who was already deep into another pile of documents. 'When did it happen?'

'Last night. Opening night tomorrow. Get it sorted out. I shall need you back here.'

'Who's in charge at the moment?'

'Some country cop. He'll meet you there.' He turned away pointedly.

Nick Verdun closed the door very quietly behind him. It was his way of dealing with irritation. It would hardly be a holiday in the country with Briggs hanging around his neck.

'Whacko!' said that young man when he heard the news. Verdun winced.

'Let's make it clear from the beginning,' he said without obvious passion, 'that we can do without juvenile expressions of delight. This a murder case. It is not a public holiday. You will need tact and diplomacy. People will be hurt.'

Briggs was nodding solemnly, his lips a little pursed to show sincerity. 'As you say, squire,' he said, changing it hastily to 'Sarge' when he caught Verdun's expression.

'Stick close to me, sunshine,' the detective said drily, 'and you may even learn something.'

If it had been a holiday, the weather could not have been better. Briggs drove through the endless miles of bush, and Nick Verdun went through the scanty paperwork. 'Who got done in?' asked Briggs.

'A middle-aged headmistress called Teresa Glencosset. Stabbed in the back with an oriental dagger—part of the décor for *Mikado*.' He waited for Briggs to say 'Micky-what?' but to his surprise the young man grinned.

'The old Mickydoo, eh? My mum used to do G and S.'

'G and S?' Verdun stared at him.

'Gilbert and Sullivan.' Briggs glanced at him. 'You don't know G and S, Sarge?'

'Not really. But you do. Well, it may come in handy.'

'*The flowers that bloom in the spring, tra-la…*' Briggs warbled, '*have nothing to do with the case…!* Appropriate, eh? *For I've got to take under my wing, tra-la…*'

'All right, all right! Save it for the bathroom.'

There was really little to learn from the notes in his hand. He preferred it that way. It was difficult working from someone else's preconceptions. Well, he doubted if it would take long to sort it out. Country people, country town mentalities—hardly the material of which complex crime is made. Which showed that Nick Verdun had done all his policing in cities, and was about to underestimate his rural cousins. He put his head back. 'Tell me when we get close. I'm going to get a bit of shut-eye. Probably won't sleep much until we get this little mess cleared up.'

The 90kph signs proclaimed the start of the town; Verdun woke as the car slowed. They drove down the main street, past the chemist's shop (Bella was cleaning a window), past Harcourt Developers (Sylvia was taking another call from the angry client), past the Tudor Tea-Shoppe (morning coffee, lunches, Devonshire teas) and the old cinema with its posters announcing '*The Mikado*'.

At the end of the street they turned and made their way back again, pulling into the theatre car-park and noting the signs of activity. The local police were there in the person of Senior Constable Pirt (who was so thankful the see Nick Verdun and Briggs that he was almost speechless), and the specialists who deal in fingerprints and the photographs of murdered corpses.

Behind him, in the doorway, an anxious elderly man with a slightly oriental cast of feature waited for officialdom to take over the burden of responsibility. Simon Lee was finding it all terribly distressing. It seemed that the murder had been committed with his antique Chinese dagger.

'Fill me in,' Verdun said once he and Pirt had shaken hands, and Simon Lee, begging to be called at any time for any reason, had made his way sadly home. 'Where's the body?'

'In here, Sergeant. I knew you wouldn't want it touched. It'll be going to Mason's—funeral directors—when we've finished with it.'

Verdun and Briggs entered the dressing room and regarded Miss Glencosset's body in silence. She was slumped forward over the bench littered with make-up and stained tissues, held in place by the chair, her head on one side.

'Gruesome, that,' said Briggs, indicating her face as it lay sightless with open eyes. 'She got half the paint off. He might have let her finish…'

'He?' Verdun gave him a cool glance. 'No preconceptions, Briggs. Plenty of women strong enough to do that.' He pointed to the dagger, sticking out rather horribly from the corpse's back.

'I thought women preferred poison.'

'You've been reading the wrong books!' He turned to Pirt. 'Who does the post-mortems down here? You can arrange that?'

Pirt, who had never had to arrange such a thing in his years as a country cop, nodded. 'The doc does police jobs. I've notified him. He'll see the body at Mason's later.'

Verdun had been looking around the bare room. 'Get him here,' he said. 'I've seen all I want for now. Is there somewhere we can sit?'

They went through the back door, across the stage, with its exotic mock-Japanese décor seeming unpleasantly tawdry in the filtered light of day, and into the Green Room. 'I can make you a cup of coffee,' Pirt said hesitantly, as if unsure of protocol where city detectives are concerned.

'Good idea.' Briggs cleared a space on a couple of chairs, and Verdun was ushered (seniority obviously being of the essence in Pirt's eyes) to the only comfortable seat, in which the Rev. Charles was normally ensconced for the same hierarchical reasons. 'Now…'

While he fiddled with the ancient urn, sorted out three mugs more or less clean from a diverse collection in a cupboard, and mixed instant coffee and (at a nod from his guests) sugar with the water which never quite boiled, he collected his thoughts, aided by a notebook that he put before him on the kitchen unit. 'No milk, I'm afraid,' he said, as put out as a hostess when the caviar hasn't arrived. 'I can send out for…'

'No need,' said Verdun. 'We don't take milk.' At another quelling glance from his boss, Briggs agreed with a respectful nod. 'Right, Constable...'

'The deceased was discovered this morning by Mr Simon Lee, the one you just met. He called a doctor and came down the street to get me. Quicker!' he explained. 'Only a coupla steps. Doc Capelli reckons she'd been dead since last night. Died straight away, he says—dagger pierced the heart. One blow, very strong. She couldn't have known much about it.' He handed the mugs round. 'Mr Lee's very upset—it's his dagger.'

'Why was she here?'

'Dress rehearsal last night. *Everybody* was here. Half the town's in the Mickydoo. And the other half comes to the performances. It's that kind of town.'

'And this teacher—Miss...?'

'Miss Glencosset. Teresa Glencosset. Head of St Chedwyn's girls' school, out on the east road.'

'Posh? Big fees and lots of extras?'

'You could say! Boarders from all over, and local farmer's girls by the day. She'd really made something of it. I remember when...'

Verdun ignored the reminiscing. 'And what was Miss Glencosset's part in the—the performance?'

'She was Katisha.'

'Katisha?'

Briggs leaned forward. 'Big contralto part. You see, the plot is that...'

'I don't think I've got time for that now, Briggs,' Verdun said crushingly. 'I'm more interested in what someone wanted to kill her for.' Briggs shrugged, as one might when faced with self-satisfied ignorance.

They took their coffee cups back into the dressing room. Nothing had been moved except the body. The dressing table was a clutter; in the centre of the chaos lay the formal, jet-black wig out of which Miss Glencosset had struggled with Natalie Percy's assistance. It lay inert, like a small, dead, fur-bearing animal.

'What on earth is that?'

'Japanese-style wig.' Briggs picked it up and was about to put it on his own head.' Verdun exploded.

'For God's sake, man, put it down! This is a murder investigation, not a charade. You might be destroying evidence.'

Briggs dropped the wig as if the small animal had developed teeth. He stood back against the wall as Verdun meandered slowly around the room, looking, touching, even sniffing, but moving nothing; then wandered away towards the door to survey the whole scene from a distance.

'Is this how you'd expect it to look?' he asked Briggs. 'After a dress rehearsal?'

'Messy? Yes.'

'It doesn't look like a struggle?'

Briggs looked around. 'Artistic chaos,' he said with some knowledge of back-stage clutter. 'My mother...'

'Your mother's experiences on stage are not a necessary part of this investigation.' Verdun was unusually cutting. He turned to Pirt. 'I want a full list of everyone connected with this production. Soonest!' Pirt, glad to have something to do, left in a whirl of country police khaki, shoving his cap on his head as he went.

'And you,' Verdun said to Briggs, fixing him with a steely gaze, 'can get out and find a couple of sandwiches. Must be somewhere close by. Meat, salad, bottle of apple juice—small. And whatever you fancy for yourself.' Briggs hesitated. 'Well?' He looked up to see the constable's hand held out in a manner suggesting money. 'Haven't you got anything on you? Then use it! You'll get it back. Keep the receipts.' He turned away. It was time to concentrate his thoughts, get the feel of the place. Sense something of what had happened here last night—begin to understand why.

Simon Lee came back with Pirt as Verdun was finishing his lunch. 'I thought it might help if I told you a little about everyone on the list,' he said nervously. 'As a stranger here you...'

'That's very thoughtful of you, sir.'

'We must get to the bottom of it,' Lee said with some desperation. 'This is a terrible thing to have happened. Such a small community. That anyone could have...' He shook his head, grieved.

'Murder is always a shocking thing,' Verdun agreed, taking the list from Pirt and placing it on a table from which he had swept music scores and rehearsal rosters. 'Right! Let's see…'

'Miss Glencosset was Katisha,' Lee began.

'Yes, I know about Miss Glencosset. What about this one—Stephen Harcourt?'

'Koko.'

'I beg your pardon?'

'Lord High Executioner.'

Verdun stared at him. 'Didn't carry his activities into private life, I suppose?' Lee gave a very pale imitation of a smile.

'He's a property developer. In quite a big way. His wife, Mary, helps with the wardrobe. Costumes, you know. Of course, we hire some. But we make as many as possible. Dulcet Merridew is our wardrobe mistress.' He pointed to her name further down the list.

'Dulcet Merridew?' Verdun pondered. 'Is that her real name or a—you know—nom-de-whatsit?'

'Oh, no, it's her real name. Sweet by name and sweet by nature.'

'Who's Michael Kowalski?'

'Local butcher. Playing the Mikado.' He saw the confusion on Verdun's face. 'You don't know the story of Mikado? The Mikado is emperor, you see. Mike is not a very impressive young man until you get him into costume, singing on stage. Then he develops quite a sense of comedy. And he has a not unpleasant voice. Odd, really, because off-stage he has no sense of humour at all.' He pointed to the next name. 'Rather like the vicar. The Reverend Charles Culbert. You'd know at once he was a churchman. Almost a stage vicar! But hide him in a costume and give him something to sing and you don't recognise him.'

It all seemed very odd to Nick Verdun: grown people dressing up and playing at being Japanese. 'What's the attraction?'

'The attraction? Well, I suppose we all have a little bit of make-believe inside us somewhere. Being a policeman, I suppose—well, inside the policeman is a real man, after all. Don't you ever feel you're playing a part?'

Verdun raised his eyebrows. 'Never thought of it that way. You're probably right.' He turned back to the list. 'Jasper and Maggie Spenlow. What do they do?'

'He's musical director. Maggie's overall director. It's her baby, if you like.'

'Husband and wife?'

'Yes. A very gifted couple.'

'Any connection with the deceased outside of Gilbert and Sullivan?'

'I really don't know. Jasper teaches part-time at St Chedwyn's. Other than that it would be difficult to assess. After all, we are all to some extent friends. A bit like a church. You know a lot of people, but some of them not very well.'

'These three?' Verdun pointed to the three little maids.

'Pattie, Natalie and Corinne. Nice little people. All St Chedwyn's students. Hardly likely to be involved in this, of course. They're young. Corinne's an art teacher, Natalie works in the check-out at the supermarket, and Pattie is still at school.'

'So they would know the deceased quite well?'

'Does one *know* one's headmistress?' Simon smiled slightly. 'Though perhaps Natalie…'

'Funny for a St Chedwyn's old girl to be working the check-outs, isn't it?'

Simon Lee shrugged. 'You know how it is with country employment. The young folk take jobs where they offer.'

They worked down the list, through the chorus to the stage hands. 'And your role?' Verdun said at last.

'I'm president. A sort of non-playing president. I'm not an actor or a singer. I have no memorising skills. But I do love Gilbert and Sullivan. They kindly acknowledged my interest by giving me a presidential hat!'

Verdun turned and faced him, letting his eyes search the older man's face in a way guaranteed to make criminals blench and even quite honest men wonder if they had been remiss over income tax. 'What do you think of all this?' he said. 'You know the people concerned, you know the intrigues and personal loves and hates. What does it all mean to you?'

Simon Lee, surviving the long stare, regarded the floor sadly, searching for words. 'It is beyond my comprehension. This is, by and large, a happy group of people. There are stresses, of course, as opening night draws closer. But it is my earnest hope that we shall discover that some stranger came in and did this vile thing. Miss Glencosset was…' he hesitated, 'well, not everybody's cup of tea, but she was a local personality respected by many within the community.' He shook his head slowly. 'I am grieved beyond measure that it should have come to this.'

Verdun nodded gravely. 'Naturally.' He stood up. 'I shall need to see you again, of course.'

'Find him!' Simon Lee blurted out, his eyes full of distress. 'Find the murderer—a small town is so very vulnerable.'

6

Pirt cleared his desk and with elephantine grace moved himself out of his office into a smaller area. If he had bothered to think it out he would probably have concluded that this visiting detective would be gone all the sooner if he had all available facilities put at his disposal; and that it wouldn't do 'im, Pirt, no 'arm at 'eadquarters if Verdun took back a good report.

Nick Verdun accepted what was offered without fuss or any irritating enquiries about how the local man would manage. He sent Briggs for another chair and placed a large pad of paper in front of each of them.

'Everything on paper. Don't go carrying things about in your head. And keep your ears and eyes wide open. Listen not only to what people say, but how they say them. Show interest but maintain your authority. I want you to interview the three girls...' He checked their names. Without looking up he detected a smirk on the other's face. 'You're here to work, Briggs. These are suspects. Not young ladies. Not until we clear them. A clever young woman can run rings round a silly young officer. Watch it! The moment they start using their eyes—you know what I mean—get suspicious.' He began to copy Lee's list on to his pad. 'And get back here as soon as you've done. If I'm not here—wait!' He looked up, suddenly and with a sharp expression that took the grin right off Briggs's face.

'Right!' said that young man. 'Right—sir!'

Verdun stood up slowly when he had finished his copying and went into Pirt's room. 'Where's Mason's? And I want to see the doctor—Capelli?'

A few minutes later he stood once more beside the dead body of Teresa Glencosset. Even with the remains of her make-up still on half the face (giving the whole thing its bizarre quality) there was something quite stately about her. He suspected that she had been a dominating personality; death in no way reduced that dignity.

Dr Capelli came in at a rush, hand outstretched to shake. 'Terrible thing,' he kept saying with an air of enjoyment, as if it had made his day. Verdun suspected that this might well be true. The constant round of tummy-aches and sore throats could hardly be called fun.

'What do you think?' he asked. The doctor lifted the sheet and moved the body so that the back was just visible. There was a neat slit where the knife had gone in. Apart from that there was little to see.

'One blow, almost certainly nicked the heart. Nothing else important. A slight laceration on the arm where she apparently scraped it when falling forward on to the dressing table. She was a heavy woman, of course. The dagger was left in.'

'Where is it?'

'Old Pirt's got it, down at the station.'

'She was halfway through taking off the war paint.' Verdun touched the cold cheek with one finger.

'Almost looks, said the doctor hesitantly, 'as if she never heard anyone come in.'

The detective stared down at the corpse. Not for the first time, he wished that the dead could speak. 'Full details as soon as possible, please.'

Briggs was waiting for him when he returned to the police station. He had several pages of copious notes. 'Saw Natalie Percy. Very shy. Could hardly squeeze a word out of her.'

'Shy? Or evasive?'

'Oh, shy, I think. Eyes down all the time.'

'Where was she last night after the rehearsal ended?'

Briggs flipped the pages over crisply. "*I left the theatre and went straight home.*" I asked her where she lived, and was she on her own? She lodges with an elderly lady on the edge of town, ten minutes' walk. No family. Bit of a loner, I think.'

'Odd, isn't it?' Verdun mused. 'Someone like that being prepared to get up on stage and act! You'd think only extroverts would want to.'

'It doesn't seem to be that way. My mother says…'

Verdun picked up a pen and started writing. 'What your mother says, Briggs, while no doubt very interesting within the family, is not part of the evidence.'

Briggs pulled a face behind his superior's back and felt better. 'Natalie must have been one of the last to see the deceased,' he offered. 'Miss Glencosset called her in just as she was going home. Asked her to help her off with the wig. She said she thought she was about the last one out of the building. Except for Mr Lee, who was waiting to lock up.'

Verdun turned thoughtfully. 'Yes. We must have another talk with Simon Lee.'

The news had travelled fast around the town. At St Chedwyn's emotions ranged from horror at the enormity of the crime ('Heaven preserve us! We shall all be killed in our beds.') to morbid excitement ('Fancy killing *Miss Glencosset!*').

Girls gathered in dormitories or slunk around outside the school trying to pick up morsels of news; the staff, shaken but not deeply stirred, managed after a wobbly start to the morning to take control and produce order out of confusion. A couple of parents arrived to take their daughters home, fearing a homicidal maniac on the loose; and among those who were less than regretful at their headmistress's demise were one or two who felt themselves filled with an almost heady relief.

The arrival of Nick Verdun with Briggs at the school did not pass unnoticed by those whose classrooms overlooked the front of the building. 'Miss!' said a number of young ladies, their hands shooting skywards, 'there's a man come—looks like a policeman. Do you think he'll want to ask us questions?'

'Don't talk nonsense, girls! Why should he want to ask *you* anything?'

Unaware of the tensions he was creating, Verdun entered the main building and found the office. Briggs, waiting as instructed with the car ('because you can't tell what young girls will get up to with an unattended car—keep your eyes open, Briggs!') was uncomfortably conscious of several heads hanging out of upstairs windows, and a sound which, to his embarrassment, could only be described as a wolf whistle.

Within the sanctum sanctorum which, until the previous night, had been Miss Glencosset's study, the deputy headmistress, Mrs Parker, faced Verdun over the desk.

'I shall have to go through Miss Glencosset's effects, of course,' he said. 'I'll try to make as little trouble and mess as possible.'

'I suppose that's necessary.' Mrs Parker, chosen for her lack of dynamic drive—for the late headmistress had disliked competition—wore a suitably grieved expression.

Verdun nodded. 'But just at this moment I would appreciate it if you would talk to me a little about her. Help me to get to know her, in a way. If her death was due to someone getting their own back, then I need to know what sort of person she was.'

'I quite understand.' Mrs Parker stared into the corner of the room, as if she saw there some clue to the dead woman's character. 'She was a good headmistress. Very efficient and good at her job. Respected, of course...'

'Why "of course"?' Verdun grinned briefly. 'I don't remember respecting *my* headmaster.'

'She had a very *powerful* personality,' Mrs Parker said earnestly. 'One had to respect.' She hesitated. 'That's not the same as liking, naturally. I don't like to speak ill…'

'Not ill,' Verdun said, quite gently. 'Truth! This is a murder investigation, Mrs Parker. Not a wake. What she was may have a real bearing on the fact that someone was sufficiently disenchanted with her to kill her.' He bent a searching gaze on her face. 'With a dagger, Mrs Parker. Into the back. Straight into the heart.' He saw her turn pale. 'To do that to someone indicates either a warped mentality or very deep hatred. So tell me the truth about Miss Glencosset.' He leaned back, encouraging her relax.

'I understand,' she said in a small voice. 'It's difficult, you see.'

'Very difficult,' said the diplomatic policeman, waiting with a kindly expression for the dam to burst.

'She *was* very efficient. And sometimes caring—in a way. But I think some of us were a little—afraid of her. There was a sort of—of coldness about her. Perhaps the word is ruthless. She knew what she wanted to make of St Chedwyn's, and nothing was going to stand in her way. Not that I blame her for that,' she said hastily. 'But it seemed kind of obsessive. Sometimes unhealthily so.'

'I know the type,' he said, nodding.

'She programmed her life, day by day, almost hour by hour. She lived out of her diary.' Mrs Parker suddenly gave a tiny smile. 'She reminded me in some way of the kind of nurse for whom hospitals would be very good places if it wasn't for the patients.'

He nodded again, soothingly. 'Did she have any particular friends on the staff?' He caught the expression on her face. 'Perhaps not the kind to make friends with subordinates? I know.' He thought, suddenly and incongruously, of Briggs. 'Any particular enemies, then?' He watched her as casually as he could, looking for giveaway flickers in the eyes, and was not disappointed.

'One or two,' she said, a trifle primly. 'She could be very hard on anyone she felt had let her down. But I don't think I'm prepared to tell you who they are,' she said with a spark of courage. 'That's their own business.'

Verdun regarded her thoughtfully, then nodded yet again. 'Fair enough. But I may have to come back to you again on that one.'

'Of course,' she said with dignity. She opened a desk drawer. 'These are Miss Glencosset's keys. I suppose it's all right to let you have them,' she said uncertainly.

'I have the authority,' he said, firmly enough to set her mind at least partially at rest. 'I shall make as little disturbance as possible.' He stood, and Mrs Parker came to her feet, taking the implied dismissal without question. As she left the room she turned.

'You'll tell me, won't you? As soon as you know. It's the parents, you see.'

'The moment I am free to inform you, I shall do so.' She closed the door behind her. 'And that,' he murmured, 'assumes that I shall be able to get to the bottom of it. Now, what have we here?'

7

Simon Lee had called a meeting of the G and S committee, consisting of himself as president, Jasper and Maggie Spenlow as directors for Mikado, Stephen and Mary Harcourt as having a particular interest in the proceedings, and Dulcet Merridew and Molly de Vance as make-weights. (Chester Parkinson, as treasurer, should have attended, but sent an acid note pointing out that not everybody could leave their responsibilities at the drop of a hat.)

They met in Simon's lounge room, and as he opened the meeting Mary suddenly gave a gasp and burst into tears.

'Oh, I'm sorry, I'm sorry!' she said through her handkerchief. 'It's been such a shock. I can't believe it...'

Her husband tutted and patted, and Maggie went to sit beside her and put an arm around her shoulders. 'My dear girl, of course it's been a terrible shock. Such a vital person, Teresa Glencosset. Impossible to think of her as dead.' She glanced up at Simon quickly, miming the act of drinking, and he poured a very small brandy and gave it to Mary.

When the emergency was over, he introduced the subject close to their hearts. 'We must decide now what to do. Sad as this dreadful business may be, we have to make up our minds whether Mikado is to go on or not.'

'It sounds so unfeeling,' Dulcet said. 'With her lying there in the—er, morgue.'

'Unfeeling or not,' Simon said, 'we open tomorrow night—or we make the decision not to.' He glanced around. 'I'd appreciate some guidance. Jasper?'

Jasper was looking tired, quite ill, Simon thought. 'It's a ghastly decision. I don't feel qualified to make it.'

'Maggie?'

'We have to be practical, don't we?' Simon agreed with her. 'Whatever we may think about it, tomorrow night has sold out already, so if we're going to cancel we have to get the news around quickly.'

'Exactly.' Simon turned to Mary Harcourt, now recovered. 'What do you think?'

Mary, her face strained and white, stared at him and then past him, looking out of the window into a carefully nurtured garden. 'What would *she* have thought?' she said at last. 'Would she want us to go on? Would she think that was very insensitive of us? What will the people round here think? Would they see it as a tribute to her, or as an insult?' She shook her head slowly. 'I don't know. I really don't.' She looked up suddenly. 'And will the police let us?'

Silence for a moment. Then Simon said, 'We've laid out a lot of money on this season.'

Dulcet, her face suddenly drawn, put her small hand flat on the coffee table at her knee. 'There's only one way we could do it with any taste. As a tribute. The show must go on! That kind of thing.' She faced Simon with a trace of belligerence. 'The money isn't the first priority.'

'I never said it was,' he said mildly. 'But it is a fact.'

'People wouldn't be shocked, would they?' Maggie said. 'Jasper, do you think they would?' He didn't answer. 'Jasper!'

'Sorry?'

'Would people be shocked if we went on with the season?'

Jasper suddenly gave an enormous yawn. 'Sorry! I haven't been sleeping very well.' He frowned, contemplating the town's reactions if they opened as planned. 'God knows!' he said at last. 'Damned if we do and damned if we don't probably.'

'Oh, very helpful!' Maggie said sarcastically. She glanced around the assembly. 'Well, I think we should go on. I think—no, I really do, Mary—I really think that Teresa would have wanted us to remember her this way. I know I would if it had been me.' She stopped quickly, facing the awful knowledge that someone in this usually genial town carried enough hate to do murder. 'At least, I think...' She trailed off, for once unsure of herself.

'Can we put it to a vote?' Simon demanded. 'We simply don't have time to discuss it at length.' And after a few minutes of well-meant hesitation it was decided unanimously that Mikado would open as planned on the following evening.

'We've forgotten one thing,' Molly said. '*Katisha* is no longer with us. That means Bella Parkinson.'

They all stared at each other. At length Simon said, 'I suppose she can do it?'

'I've had her understudying.' Jasper roused himself. 'She'll be better than nothing.' He turned to his wife. 'Will you tell her or shall I?'

'We'll go together,' Maggie said. 'She may need resuscitation!'

Chester Parkinson was loath to leave his shop, but he was not prepared to let Bella be interviewed on her own. Jasper and Maggie were ushered through into the sitting room behind the pharmacy, where Bella was taken by surprise with an iron in her hand.

'We thought it best to come rather than ring,' Maggie said, taking the initiative. 'You've heard the dreadful news, of course.'

'Indeed we have.' Chester looked grim. Bella actually seemed as if she might have been having a little weep in memory of the dead Katisha.

'Well, we've come to let you know...'

'Right after the dress rehearsal like that!' Bella said. 'How could anyone?'

'One really wonders where the police are these days.' Chester was full of righteous civic wrath.

Jasper snorted. 'My dear Parkinson, they could hardly be expected to *guess…*'

'So we thought it right to come,' Maggie tried once more.

'To let us know. How kind of you.' Chester was unusually gracious.

'Yes.' Maggie looked faintly surprised. 'We wanted you to have plenty of warning.'

'Warning?'

'Cancellation,' Bella said, nodding ruefully. 'Well, we had expected it, of course.'

Maggie shook her head vehemently. 'No! Not at all. The committee decided unanimously that we should go on. Miss Glencosset would have expected it. So, Bella…'

Bella stared at her in anguish, her hand to her cheek. She turned quite pale, as if she might faint; Chester held out a hand to her instinctively.

'Oh, no—she couldn't do that,' he said, shaken out of his usual passivity. 'My wife couldn't possibly…'

'But she's understudy,' Maggie said impatiently. 'She knows the part. She's got the voice—I think.' She looked at Bella, whose face was warming gently, like colour flooding a black and white film. Had she got the voice? It didn't matter! Bella would have to go out there and do something—anything. The alternative was cancellation. 'Bella…'

'No, Maggie!' Chester said firmly; and Bella, seeing his face, knew that she should agree, stand meekly a little way behind his shoulder, let him make the decisions. It had always been thus. 'Bella can't…'

Then Bella, filled with a sudden inexplicable exuberance of spirit, felt herself take a step forward. And a voice she barely recognised came up from her chest, through her larynx, vibrated across tongue and lips, and brought a rictus of surprise to her husband's face.

'Of course I'll do it, Maggie dear,' she said, her voice deepening, strengthening, almost as if Miss Glencosset were using her as a mouthpiece. ('I *am* Teresa Glencosset!' she told herself in wonder. 'I am strong. And I *can* do it.').

Maggie, relieved out of all proportion, leaned forward and kissed her cheek. 'Beaut lady!' she exclaimed. 'You're a doll! Have a run-through with Jasper. You'll wow them!'

Chester, watching his wife picking up the iron as if it were a sword, suffered an internal sensation like a small earthquake. He had an unwelcome feeling that something irrevocable had just taken place.

'I hope we made the right choice,' Simon Lee was saying to Verdun. 'It was unanimous. And somehow...' He pondered for a moment. 'Yes, all in all, and in consideration of the kind of duty-bound woman Teresa Glencosset was, it *was* the right choice. I've no doubt she would have done the same in our place.' He glanced at the detective. 'You're not going to stop us, are you?'

Verdun shook his head. 'We've been over the theatre pretty thoroughly, and the dressing room is now open for use. So—tomorrow's the night! Well, may I wish you all the very best? It won't be easy under the circumstances. Have you had any reactions?'

'Not yet.' He smiled faintly. 'It would be out of order to assume that we may have our first total sell-out on our hands. People are by nature ghoulish.'

'And you have someone to replace the—Miss Glencosset?'

The smile disappeared. 'Ah yes. Bella Parkinson. Well, we must hope for the best.' He shrugged philosophically. 'What can I do for you?'

'You lock up after the rehearsals, I believe?'

'I do.'

'Always?'

'Always. I hold the keys. My interest as president is not as a performer, you see. I see to the things that the—the more artistic find trying to remember. Like locking up! And putting things away.' He nodded gently.

'A scatter-brained lot?' Verdun said sympathetically.

'Not so much scatter-brained. Brains full of other things, I suppose.'

'So you locked up last night?' Lee nodded, his face suddenly solemn. 'What was the state of things in the theatre?'

'I had checked the front doors, where the audience would come in.' He frowned, recalling his movements. 'They lock with a key and have bolts top and bottom. Then I went backstage—through the auditorium, you understand?—and checked that all the lights were off.'

'And they were?'

'Yes. There's one by the Green Room door, leading to the car-park, which has to be switched off separately. And there's a security switch that has to be set. But all other lights were off.'

'Dressing rooms?'

'Yes, those as well. The doors were slightly open, and I would have seen if there had been...' He stopped. 'I assumed...'

'Assume nothing,' said Verdun drily. 'Not in a murder case.'

'Do you think it had already happened? I thought someone must have come back.'

'Would she have been sitting in the dark, listening to you locking up?' Verdun shook his head. 'The murderer chose his time. An opportunist! It sounds as if it must have happened while you were at the front of the theatre. How long did it take you to lock the doors?'

'Perhaps five minutes. I wasn't in a hurry. I heard nothing.'

'She probably died instantaneously.'

'Thank God for that, anyway.' Simon Lee closed his eyes for a moment. 'Forgive me—it's hard to take in. You mean that someone—someone who was here already—one of us...?'

'It looks like it.' Verdun's eyes were sympathetic.

'...picked up my dagger and went in there while she was removing her makeup...' He gave a deep sigh. 'What if I had come back more quickly than I did?'

'Who knows? No murder—or perhaps two murders!'

'Not someone off the street?' His eyes were pleading.

'I don't think so. Such tight timing. Between the last person going out—that seems to be Natalie Percy, apart from yourself—and you locking the theatre doors. And finding time to notice the dagger—oh, no, it's not possible. This, I'm afraid, is a much more *personal* killing. Someone really didn't like Miss Teresa Glencosset.'

Simon Lee, looking drawn and suddenly very Chinese, nodded like a mandarin. 'Well, we must face it, I suppose.' He glanced up, embarrassed. 'Do you have any—any theories?'

'Not yet.' Verdun put on his 'official' face. 'But I shall have a much better idea of things in a day or two.'

'I wonder if you would like a ticket for tomorrow's opening? I do have a few kept back for emergencies. Or is that altogether too macabre?'

Verdun hesitated, then smiled. 'Thank you. I'll come. Can you make it two? My young constable, Briggs, was apparently brought up on Mikado.'

'My pleasure!' Simon rose to his feet and made a note on his pad. 'They'll be at the box office for you.' He paused for a moment, his expression all at once lengthening into sadness. 'I should be most obliged if you would keep me in touch with developments. As president, you understand…'

'Of course.' Verdun stood and moved towards the door. 'And you, Mr Lee, will please bring to me any information you may acquire. For instance,' he said with his hand on the doorknob, 'is there anyone who would gain in any way from a cancellation of the season? Or anyone who simply wouldn't care one way or the other?'

Lee lifted his shoulders, spread his hands. 'Not to my knowledge. I should have said this was a very keen society.'

'But *someone* didn't care,' Verdun said firmly, looking into the old man's eyes with intensity. 'Someone was prepared to take the chance. I wonder who?'

8

The Reverend Charles Culbert might well have been considering the state of his ill-kept garden, standing by his study window with an air of abstraction. He was in fact contemplating the evils that men do.

Miss Glencosset's funeral would take place on the following Monday morning in his church (police permitting), to be concluded by cremation in a private ceremony to be attended only by himself and a couple of very distant cousins who had hopes of largesse from the deceased woman's will. He wondered what he could possibly say about this dynamic woman; he was finding her as terrifying in death as she had been in life, making demands on him that he feared he could not meet, eyeing him even from the— well, not the grave, yet, but from Mason's funeral chapel.

It was widely held that, while she filled her position in the school and the town with appropriate grace and competence, Miss Glencosset had not been a particularly *nice* person. He could concur; recent encounters had left him alarmed and dismayed. Nevertheless, he had a duty to the dead, and so he must find something to say that would, perhaps, heal some of the hurt of the past days, let people start again without anger and a lack of trust. For he saw, in the main street and in places where local folk foregathered, that this murder had brought to the surface many of the less attractive aspects of human nature.

He had pondered on 'Judge not, that ye be not judged,' and 'Let him who is without sin…' but these carried a kind of rebuke to the murdered woman, and it must not be thought by anyone (and especially not by the murderer) that one could shift blame for such a heinous act by turning it on to the victim. However much she might have 'asked for it', Miss Glencosset was entitled to a decent and respectful disposal.

Even more disconcerting was the knowledge (for the detective was adamant that this was no 'outside job') that one of his parishioners had seen fit to take justice into his (her?) own hands. Unreasonably, he hoped it wasn't a woman. Women, he knew, were demanding complete equality with men, but surely this was a most unwomanly act? One that the most vehement feminist would not wish to claim on sexist grounds. He brought his roving mind back to realities. But there was a murderer; and it was someone he knew! Someone with a mind out of balance? With hidden anger or fear or a threatened self-interest creating a confusion of thought? He cast his mind around the parish, but he had to conclude that apart from old Jake Brewster out at Plumley's Farm he knew no one who could easily be categorised as 'mad'. And even old Jake wasn't dangerous.

Someone was knocking on the front door. He went along the dark passageway and let in a flood of blinding sunlight, to reveal the dust of Mrs Bedwell's slap-dash cleaning methods. Nick Verdun and Briggs stood on the step. 'Have you a moment?' the sergeant was saying, as Culbert took a deep breath to steady a sudden flurry in his chest.

'Come in, come in!' he cried in a piece of what he recognised as shockingly bad acting. Verdun, taken aback by the warmth, entered the clammy hallway.

'We met briefly,' Verdun was saying as Culbert led the way into a large sitting room that had the slightly gritty appearance of a room rarely used and imperfectly cleaned. 'I'm trying to get round to as many as I can today...'

'Very wise,' said the cleric. '*Very* wise! A cup of something?' He gazed around vacantly, as if expecting a tea-pot to appear from nowhere. 'Perhaps sherry?'

'Not on duty, thank you, sir.' Verdun sat down.

'Oh, do sit down. Is that chair comfortable? Perhaps this one? Or over there—the light's better over there.' He could hear himself rambling on and on, and took a sharp hold on his tongue. Too much chattering could be misconstrued as guilty nerves. 'How can I help?'

Verdun, regarding him thoughtfully, took out a pen and his notebook. Behind him, in an even less comfortable chair, Briggs did the same. Culbert swallowed to clear a very nervous throat.

'I'm checking out everyone's movements after the dress rehearsal last night. When you left the theatre, sir, who was still there?'

The Rev Charles looked thoroughly alarmed. 'Oh, my goodness! Oh dear! My memory, you know—it's not the best. I doubt if I even noticed at the time.'

'Try to think, please. Place yourself, say, in the Green Room, after you had taken off your costume.' He watched the contortions of the vicar's eyebrows as they joined in the search for truth.

'Hung it up,' Culbert said, picturing the scene. 'Removed makeup. Washed my hands—the makeup is quite heavy,' he explained, momentarily embarrassed at what the detective might be thinking. 'Spoke briefly to one or two. Some had already gone. Dulcet Merridew was busy, Mary was helping her to check costumes. Very difficult to recall...' He shrugged apologetically.

'Anything unusual about the evening? Outside the normal stresses of a dress rehearsal, that is.'

'Well...' Culbert hesitated, pursing his lips and frowning. 'Perhaps not too unusual. But there had been rather a lot of frayed tempers recently. I don't quite know why. After all, Mikado is well-known, fun to do...' His mournful expression belied the comment. 'It should have been, as the children say, a doodle.'

'Doddle,' said Verdun.

'Ah!' For a moment the taut expression relaxed. 'I should never make the attempt to move with the times. I invariably get it wrong.'

Verdun grinned. 'You need a computer to keep up with colloquial English among the young these days.'

The vicar nodded slowly. 'I'm afraid *computer* is a dirty word to me. Microchips! Sounds more like a very small fried potato. I don't know where we're all going, I'm sure.'

'Murder hasn't changed much over the centuries,' Verdun said with asperity, and the Rev Charles glanced at him quickly.

'I couldn't do your job, Mr Verdun,' he said humbly. 'I might rage over the taking of a life, but I couldn't bring myself to accuse another human being of such wickedness.'

Verdun felt mildly annoyed. 'Someone has to do it. Should we ignore crime and vice in case we get our hands dirty?'

'No, no, no! You are, of course, absolutely right. I fear I am a moral coward.' He smiled gently. 'I was speaking of my own weakness, not your strength.'

The detective looked directly at him. 'Tell me about Teresa Glencosset. How long have you known her?'

It seemed to be another tricky question. Culbert frowned. 'How long has she been here?'

'About twelve years, according to Mrs Parker at the school. Seven years as deputy, five as headmistress.'

'Then I have known her for twelve years. I called on her when she first moved into a small house in town, before she went out to the headmistress's house.'

'Was she a church-goer?'

Another hesitation. 'Of the kind who attends regularly as a social grace without letting it become too much a part of life.' It was the nearest he could come to a condemnation. 'She was there every Sunday morning, sitting near the front, with her girls a few rows behind.'

'Compulsory church parade?'

'Oh, dear me, no. Those days are gone for ever, Mr Verdun. My confirmation candidates were expected to attend as a part of their course. And there were others who came because they wanted to. And others, I believe, who came because of the choirboys!' He raised an eyebrow significantly.

'Does that still go on?' Verdun asked, grinning.

'Oh, indeed! The attraction of—ah—adolescent flesh to flesh is very strong, and choirboys seem to be able to exert it, even in these liberated times.'

'Tell me,' said Verdun, 'was Michael Kowalski there when you left?'

Culbert suffered a shamefully wicked hope that the butcher might be The One. The moment the thought popped into his head he tried to obliterate it. That was true sin—to turn a man into a murderer, even as a theory, because it would remove him from Molly's orbit. He offered a hasty prayer of confession, hoping that absolution would follow.

'He was still there,' he said haltingly. 'Yes, I can say that he was still there.' Fawning all over Molly! That was how he could be so sure.

'And...' Verdun referred to his notes, 'Miss de Vance?' He glanced towards the vicar, who was shifting uncomfortably in his chair.

'*He knows!*' Culbert was thinking wildly. '*Someone has spoken!*' Was it, he wondered, a possible motive for murder? Could one be arrested simply for having fallen for a desirable little woman for the first time in one's life? Surely not!

'Yes,' he said, his voice strained. 'Miss de Vance was there too.'

'Did they leave together?'

'I believe they may have done.' He took off his spectacles and polished them furiously.

'If so, and if you can vouch for them, then that presumably leaves them in the clear?'

'But they might have separated outside the theatre,' Culbert's wicked demon said quickly. 'I couldn't vouch for that.'

'That's true.' Verdun ran his eye down the notes. He had nothing more to ask at the moment, but the interview had been more rewarding than he had expected. He sensed a deep disturbance somewhere within the clerical garb. It might be a good idea to find out what it was all about. Wearing the cloth did not make a man immune from the sins of the world; no one knew that better than an experienced policeman.

'Funny,' said Verdun suddenly, relaxing as he prepared to leave, 'I always thought of the country as a haven of peace. Shows how much a townie knows.'

Culbert escorted them to the front door, letting in the sunshine once more and standing out on the porch with his eyes half closed against the powerful light. 'The country,' he said slowly, 'has no claim on virtue. One lives close—to the land, to each other. One relies on one's neighbours in a way that town people no longer do. And this is at once a strength and a weakness. In a city one could pretend this—this calamity had not happened, unless one was personally involved. Here...' He gazed around him as if he saw the tall trees, the wide hectares of land, the cluster of houses that was the basis of this rural community, for the first time.

'Here, there is nowhere that one can avoid it. We are, as it were, a part of each other. And sometimes,' he turned to stare at the detective, 'it can be painful. Very painful, Mr Verdun. In a way that cities have forgotten.' He stopped. 'Good day to you!'

Verdun regarded the suddenly closed door with surprise. What was it like to be the shepherd of the flock in this backwater? What might it do to a man who was too vulnerable, whose sensitivity either brought him out or, in this case apparently, drove him in on himself? He walked down the driveway to the car. Was there any truth, he asked himself, in the rumour he had heard about the vicar and Molly de Vance, whom he had not yet interviewed?

Briggs opened the car door. 'A bit like the bishop and the actress,' Verdun said inconsequentially as he got in. Briggs, starting the car, said 'Beg yours?' But the detective shrugged.

'The Spenlows,' he said. 'Get on with it, Macduff!'

Jasper was marking some music tests when Nick Verdun rang the bell; Maggie was relaxing with a book now that her part in the production was over with the end of the dress rehearsal. Neither was in a hurry to answer the door. When Jasper, at Maggie's strident request, went to see who was there, Verdun was interested to see a strangely pugnacious hardening of the chin line. He flashed his ID and Jasper glanced at it without really seeing it. Briggs followed them inside.

'You'd better come in,' Jasper said without warmth. 'This is a nasty business.'

'It is indeed.' He moved ahead of Jasper into a high-ceilinged room full of character. 'Nice place. I like these old houses. Did you have to do much to it?'

Jasper relaxed a little. 'You know something about renovations?'

'A little. I inherited a run-down little place from my aunt. Took me a couple of years to get it right. Then I had to sell it.'

'Why?'

'The powers-that-be moved me.'

'Tough,' said Jasper. 'Maggie! It's the detective—sorry, I forget your name.'

'Nick Verdun. Detective Sergeant. And Constable Briggs.' He suspected that the loss of memory was a ploy on Jasper's part to keep him in his place. Well, he'd play the game! It might bring something out into the open.

Maggie arrived with a high-nosed look about her that told him he was intruding. Nerves, he had often said, took people in many different ways. He smiled in friendly fashion and she indicated a chair next to the table. 'You'll want to take notes, no doubt.'

He wondered if it would be going too far to say 'Ar, missus,' and pull his forelock. Instead, he sat himself comfortably and put the notebook where it would be handy but not too intrusive. Briggs stood stolidly near the wall, until Maggie, impatiently, waved him to a chair.

'I'm checking up on where everyone was at the end of last night's rehearsal,' Verdun began. 'Would you be good enough to tell me what happened after the rehearsal ended?'

In general, the story they told matched everyone else's. Maggie had, she said, thrown her script across the Green Room in a fit of exuberance, and then let someone, she couldn't recall who, make her a cup of coffee. From then on it had been one long relaxation, talking nineteen to the dozen, waiting (interminably, she implied) for Jasper to be ready so that they could go home and sleep it off.

Nick Verdun turned to Jasper. 'And you, sir?'

'Much the same, of course. Except that I had a few places in my orchestral score where alterations had to be made. So I found myself a quiet corner...'

'Quiet, in that chaos?' Maggie said quite acidly; and Verdun watched them even more carefully for what was not being said.

'Quietish.' Jasper kept his voice level, not looking at her. 'It took me about fifteen minutes, then I put the music away in the cupboard, then...'

'By that time,' Maggie interrupted, 'just about everyone had gone. I decided to get some fish and chips. We hadn't eaten properly all day. So I went down the street—it's about fifty yards, well, metres, I suppose. Corinne was with me, one of the 'three little maids'—do you know Mikado?'

'I'm getting to.' Verdun grinned. 'How long were you?'

'Ten minutes. Not more. They're very quick, and there was no one else in there.' She glanced up at him. 'Except Corinne,' she said deliberately, establishing not only her own alibi but also the fact that she knew she needed one.

'And meanwhile...?' He turned to Jasper, who shrugged.

'I finished what I was doing, made sure the cover was on the electronic keyboard, said goodnight to—somebody, I don't remember who, then went outside to wait for Maggie.'

She nodded. 'He was there when I got back.'

'Anyone else around?'

Maggie frowned. 'Not by then, I suppose. Oh, Simon must have been somewhere. We drove home quickly and ate the fish and chips. That's all. Will it do?'

'Were you the last out, sir?' Verdun asked Jasper.

'Oh, I doubt it. I really don't remember too clearly, but I would think there were others around.'

Verdun made a few brief notes in his book. He was intrigued. The atmosphere in the pleasant room, in spite of all the tastefulness and the good furniture, was chilly. He didn't think it was because he was there. It was noticeable that husband and wife never really looked at each other, though they gave the impression of working together. He wondered what passions flowed through the cleverly renovated house.

'That was all right,' Jasper said after he had shown the visitors out. 'Doesn't look especially bright to me.'

Maggie narrowed her eyes. 'I don't know. I had the feeling that he was perhaps seeing more than we were revealing.'

Jasper gave a harsh laugh. 'Oh, very enigmatic! You should write a book.'

'Perhaps I will,' she said. 'One day.'

9

Bella regarded her husband with a solicitous eye. He was taking her sudden rise to prominence quite strangely, hardly speaking to her or listening to what she was saying. Naturally enough, she would like to have been able to discuss it with him; but there was a dour look about him that made that kind of intimacy impossible. She sighed. Well, men had a lot on their minds, she knew that. If Mother had taught her nothing else, she had certainly drummed that into her. It was why her father had died of cirrhosis of the liver, driven to drink by the vicissitudes of everyday living.

Only recently had she begun to wonder why her mother, who had carried not only the household but their little business on her shoulders, had not found it necessary to drink the problems away.

'Chester,' she had said hesitantly, 'you don't *mind* me doing Katisha, do you?'

He had been almost rude. 'Mind? Why should I mind? Presumably you think you can do it. What's it got to do with me?' And, when she had foolishly pressed on: 'I have other things on my mind, Bella. *Real* things! If you want to cavort on stage and make a fool of yourself, that's up to you.'

She had almost cried then; but long practice held, and she went up to their bedroom and sang (under her breath) a few lines of Katisha's music, and at once felt better. She would never go against Chester. He was a wonderful man, and she cared for him greatly. But a tiny door had opened in her mind, a door unnoticed by her husband, a door which had her name on it, quite alone. Not *Mrs Chester Parkinson,* but *Bella Parkinson, singer!* Without analysing it too deeply, she felt she would be prepared to fight—just a little—to keep that door open.

Chester, downstairs, was grappling with the shop accounts; when he had finished those he would have to tackle the G and S books; then, perhaps, he would be able to see his way clear.

There were stickers on all the Mikado posters scattered around the town. *'OPENING TONIGHT!'* they proclaimed. Simon Lee and a small flock of helpers had spent the early hours from 6 a.m. with pots of paste and strips of paper hastily hand-written. By shop-opening time there were small groups around the posters in the main street, discussing the pros and cons of 'the show must go on'. It was probably the best publicity the society had ever had.

Inside the theatre there was an orgy of cleaning and organisation. Everyone not tied to a daytime job was there; costumes were pressed and hung up and the sound of vacuum cleaners could be heard everywhere. It was a blessing that there was so much to do; only when an involuntary coffee break was called by one group or another did the matter closest to their hearts get an airing.

When Verdun and Briggs entered through the back door a sudden silence fell. The theatre became a place of eyes, all turned on the detective, who was used to it and so in no way fazed by being the centre of attention. It often struck him as odd that he was arbitrarily brought into such contact with people he had never met and would probably never see again once the case was closed, and that their attitude not infrequently was one of antagonism. He was, after all, only doing his job. Briggs, less used to it, felt the coolness and stood well back, by the door.

'Good day,' Verdun said, looking around him for the one who appeared to be in charge. This turned out to be Maggie, who said 'Oh...' in a bored tone of voice and asked him what he wanted.

'We are rather busy, as you can see,' she said, vaguely indicating the complete cessation of activity.

He glanced about him. 'So I see,' he said, smiling cheerfully. 'I just wanted to look at the dressing room again.'

'It was a frightful nuisance when we couldn't use it. I hope you're not going to keep us out again. You will hurry up and finish with it, won't you?'

Verdun nodded. 'Murder is a frightful bore,' he agreed, and was interested to see that she turned a little red.

He and Briggs stood in the dressing room, searching it for the last time with their eyes, and picking up the odd piece of cotton wool or tissue that had been left behind. 'This can't tell us anything else,' Verdun said at last. 'I wanted to be sure. Tell them we shan't want it again.'

He wandered out of the theatre into the car-park. By night it was full of pools of shadow—he knew this because he had taken the trouble late on the previous evening, before retiring to bed in the Imperial Hotel, to look for himself. There was a light outside the stage door, controlled from the inside; one at each corner of the parking space; and one at the entry from the street. Enough to show you where your car was, but plenty of shadowy areas where one could stand and be virtually unseen. So had someone slipped in from the outside and stabbed Teresa Glencosset in an amazingly convenient moment when no one else was near the dressing room? He still doubted it, but it had to be taken into account.

It seemed likely that nothing much could be done while the entire production was getting itself together; so he bought a couple of sandwiches and a can of beer each and told Briggs to head out beyond the town for a spot where they could commune with nature and ponder the facts of the case as they knew them. Briggs looked nervous at the idea of 'communing'; but when Verdun told him to pull up in a road-side parking place commanding a wonderful view of the surrounding countryside he began to get the hang of it, and switched off the engine and opened his door so that the cool breeze could blow in.

'It makes you wonder,' said Verdun, through a massively constructed bread roll with roast beef, salad and mayonnaise all spilling out on to his shirt front, 'why we spend our lives in the towns and cities, cut off from all this kind of thing.' He waved an expansive hand, losing a lettuce leaf in the process.

Briggs stared about him. 'All right for a holiday, I suppose,' he said at last. 'Drive you mad to live in it!'

'Why?'

Briggs struggled with his analysis of country life. 'Well, Sarge,' he said finally, 'for one thing, there aren't that many murders. Wouldn't do *you* much good.'

'I don't demand murders for a happy life,' Verdun protested. 'I daresay there are other things I could do. Farming, perhaps.'

'Drive you potty in a week,' Briggs said wisely. 'The reason you like this is because it's not something you see all that often. You wouldn't like to get like that lot, would you?' he added, popping open his beer can.

'What's wrong with them?'

'Crackers, all of them! No idea. Out of touch.' He opened his mouth and inserted a wedge of tuna sandwich with gherkins.

'So you think I'm a townie, do you?'

'No doubt of it—Sarge!' He grinned at his superior. 'You and me both. Not enough villains in the country. Besides—you might get to be like old Pirt!'

'Ah.' Verdun said. He gazed across the wide, rolling panorama of paddock and bush, hill and valley, and sighed. 'Such wisdom from one so young. Well, we'd better get back to work. Get rid of the horrible looking thing.' He was referring to the tuna sandwich, now threatening to slide on to the youngster's lap.

Briggs shoved it into his mouth and was heard to ask, in muffled tones, 'Where to?'

'The school, I think. I'll spend the afternoon going through Miss Glencosset's diaries.

'And me?'

'Ah, yes. Well, how would you like to spend a happy hour or so drifting aimlessly around the town and picking up whatever gossip you can? Going on with Mikado will have annoyed some and pleased others. They may therefore be readier than usual to talk. Just get the feel of the place, Briggs. And at some point ring back to HQ and see if there's been any kind of similar crime in the area in the past few years. I don't think we're looking for an outsider, but you never know.'

'Sarge!' Briggs put the car at the hill down which lay the school as if he were taking part in a rally. Verdun, refusing to show alarm at their progress, kept his mouth tight shut. But when they arrived at the school gates he said, 'Put me down here. We don't want to kill any absconding schoolgirl, do we?'

Briggs grinned. 'Your nerves are good! My mother would've stopped me a mile back.'

Verdun, his feet now safely on the ground, turned slightly towards the young man. 'I am not your mother, Briggs. Fortunately for both of us.' He emerged from the car and stood, regarding the school frontage. 'Don't antagonise the natives by making them jump for their lives.'

Briggs revved the engine. 'No worries, sir. I'll drive like my aunt Kate.'

'Your family appears to be taking over.' Verdun banged on the car roof, and watched the car disappear in a cloud of dust from the verge, along the road into town.

Mrs Parker had left orders that he should have complete freedom in Miss Glencosset's rooms. The maid who let him in regarded him with a mixture of interest and alarm, and he smiled at her and thanked her courteously, closing the door after her with enough old-world charm to send her back to her mates in quite a tizzy. The fact that he was moderately good-looking and had a certain air of authority had not been lost on the domestics.

He stood in the centre of the study, absorbing an atmosphere enhanced by good furniture tastefully arranged. This was a billet for life, he imagined; and indeed it had been. One would have to offend governors and townspeople *and* the staff to lose such a headship.

One side of the room held a mighty bookcase, jarrah and brass, filled from top to bottom with well-bound books. Verdun wandered over and inspected a few titles. Dickens and Thackeray, Kingsley Amis, Dorothy L Sayers, a presentation Chaucer, a dozen or so modern authors: the 'English' shelf, he surmised. There were American books, too; some Thomas Mann representing Germany; Miles Franklyn, getting closer to home; a 'Banjo' Paterson collection; and a whole shelf of reference books, dictionaries, historical events, and a thesaurus—enough to start a book shop, he thought. Though not, on the whole, it seemed, the collection of an intellectual.

At one side were bound copies of the Gilbert and Sullivan operas; he took out Mikado and riffled through it. Like a foreign language, it seemed to him, lines and dots and Italian phrases; he wondered that anyone had patience enough to learn to read music. He moved on further; and at the end of the shelf he came across the diaries, those personal details that had been Teresa Glencosset's leisure activity, her link with past and future. Verdun took out the most recent and sat himself in her comfortable chair.

When Briggs returned to the school at nearly four-thirty he found Verdun still sitting in the chair, deep into the private life of the deceased Katisha. Glancing up with a start of surprise, he said, 'Good lord, is that the time?' He looked down at the book in his hand and closed it slowly. 'Briggs, I think we have an interesting case here.'

'Found something good, have you, Sarge?'

'Found something, yes.' He returned the diary to its place on the shelf. 'But I doubt if it's good.' He followed the younger man out to the car, turning back to look at the school, rosy in the declining sunlight. 'I doubt very much if it's good, Briggs.'

Nick Verdun had arranged for Constable Pirt to be present backstage. He had no reason to believe that further murders were planned, but it was as well to be sure. A few of the cast looked askance at the burly figure in uniform; but he kept his place, as nervous of getting caught up in anything theatrical as they presumably were of being personally involved in the current investigation.

The Green Room was a seething mass of people an hour and a half before the performance was due to start. Some were half dressed, partially made up, wandering in search of coffee or hoping to locate some item of costume temporarily gone missing. Dulcet Merridew and Mary Harcourt sped between the bodies, their arms full of clothes; and Maggie Spenlow, now relieved of direct action, called in to wish them well and then disappeared in the direction of the Imperial Hotel's more exclusive bar.

Jasper watched her go, then got down to the serious business of ensuring the musical success of the evening. He had taken Bella Parkinson through 'Katisha's' role in the afternoon, and though she would hardly strike the audience as the dynamically powerful figure of Miss Glencosset would have done, she would do well enough. In fact, he had been quite taken aback by her intensity.

'You've been hiding your light under a bushel,' he had said, and she, surprisingly, had laughed quite gaily.

'It's an ill wind...'

For a moment he had not understood. When he did, he felt a sudden jolt; if Teresa Glencosset's door had closed, it was perhaps right that Bella's should have opened. He wondered if it made the ugliness of this death in some way less terrible.

For Senior Constable Pirt, standing in semi-official manner by the wall, the goings-on backstage were proving a revelation. As he took up his position the place had been full of people he knew; but as time drew on, slowly, almost imperceptibly, the figures were those of strangers, and Japanese strangers at that. The faces, white-painted, and the starkly black wigs gave the whole thing such an air of unreality that he was suddenly not surprised that murder should have been done in this place. Constrained by the stiff costumes, men and women even walked with a different gait.

And as curtain-up came closer a nervous silence fell upon the theatre.

At the front, where the box office was being besieged by a long queue, excitement was intense though controlled. No one liked to voice the thought that was in every mind: that the murder had been very good for business. No one, that is, but Chester Parkinson, standing to one side, his face still drawn and slightly irritable. It was assumed (though who would be game to comment on that?) that he was not too pleased about Bella's sudden rise to prominence.

'Ghouls!' he was saying to Maggie, who had returned from the hotel nicely warmed and ready for anything. 'You'll see—it'll be full every night.' He snorted derisively. 'What shall we arrange for next year?'

Maggie looked at him with one eyebrow up. 'Whatever do you mean, Chester?' She grinned slyly. 'You should be jolly pleased to see full houses.'

He turned quickly to catch her expression. 'I'm not sure I like that.'

She was surprised that he seemed angry. 'Good for the account book!'

'What are you implying?' He glared at her.

'Good heavens, man! I'm not implying anything. You're as touchy as a prima donna. What is it? Bella's debut? You don't have to be nervous. She'll do OK. Jasper's been working with her.'

Chester, mumbling something she didn't quite catch, moved away and went into the theatre, and she watched him go. A sudden thought came to her, and gave her no comfort. First night nerves under the present conditions might be construed as something more.

The house lights dimmed; the orchestra thumped into the opening chords of the overture. As the curtains parted, Bingo Rafferty's scenery brought a spatter of applause, and the mock-Japanese music led into the first chorus. An almost tangible sense of relaxation took place as the audience settled down to enjoy something most of them already knew. Lolly papers were crackled, a party from an old folks' home whispered piercingly across the aisle, and at the back of the theatre Nick Verdun sat next to young Briggs and waited to be enlightened.

'Who's that?' he muttered as an unrecognisable Nanki-Poo crossed the stage.

'Nanki-Poo.'

'No, I mean *who* is it?'

'Oh—Dave Shafto. Have you seen him yet?'

'Not properly.'

A woman in front of them turned and shushed them quite violently. Anything but reverential concentration was clearly not on. Lowering his voice even further, he said, 'I'll see him tomorrow.' Briggs grinned foolishly towards the stage and nodded. Outplayed, Verdun capitulated and, leaning as far back as was possible in a very uncomfortable seat, gave himself over to the performance.

The appearance of Pooh-Bah brought a flurry of movement and whispering with it. 'It's the vicar!' could be heard as programmes were consulted in the light from the stage. Verdun watched with fascinated awe. The exotically garbed figure, pompously well-padded around the abdomen, was so unlike the gangling man of God whom Verdun had briefly met as to be astonishing.

'Good Lord!' the detective said, and the woman in front of him turned and shushed him again.

'*She'll toddle away, as all aver*', warbled the Rev Charles in a not at all unpleasing light baritone voice, '*with the Lord High Executioner!*'

Briggs chuckled, and Verdun turned to stare. The young man was totally involved with what was happening on stage, leaning forward slightly, his face ready to reflect the emotions of a bunch of local nobodies dressed up in garish dressing gowns and wearing funny wigs. It was beyond Verdun's comprehension.

When Stephen Harcourt trotted on to the boards there was a stirring round of applause; whether for the character or for the man inside the clothes it was impossible to tell. '*Taken from the county jail*,' sang the property developer with quite a lively line in wicked glances at the audience, *'by a set of curious chances; Liberated then on bail, on my own recognizances...'*

Verdun shifted on his hard seat. 'If you're the one I'm after, my friend,' he murmured (but to himself, not to disturb the woman in front), 'There'll be no bail! And if you're seeing yourself as lord high executioner outside this building you've got another think coming.'

Briggs poked him suddenly. 'This is really funny,' he said, not wishing his superior to miss a single moment of delight. His eyes went back to the stage, a wide anticipatory grin on his face. Koko, the Lord High Executioner, Stephen Harcourt of Harcourt Developers, was unleashing a veritable toilet-roll of paper that ran about all over the stage and was greeted with a roar of laughter.

'As someday it may happen that a victim must be found,' he leered at the people in the front rows, *'I've got a little list...!'* Verdun listened carefully; much of the list's contents left him cold, but he could tell from the reactions of the audience that there were many local references: councillors, he imagined, and authority figures known to a farming population.

Who would he, Verdun, put on a list of miscreants who would 'never be missed'? Murderers, generally, though he had known a few for whom he had had pity rather than anger; vandals and young fools who thought it was fun to put telephone boxes out of order; old fools who drove in the middle of the road at sixty kilometres an hour and were blind enough not to notice the pile-up of traffic behind them.

Child abusers! He'd put *them* on the list. He'd had to help clear up the mess. His mind came slowly round to the present investigation. What he had been reading in Miss Glencosset's study almost persuaded him that she would have gone high on his list. But someone else had beaten him to it! Someone, perhaps backstage at this moment, perhaps simply sitting there in the auditorium, brooding on past angers, had made a list with only one name on it—and carried out the Lord High Executioner's role.

Then Verdun sat up suddenly with a jolt. 'List' implied more than one name! He stared glumly at the lighted stage, where a bevy of Japanese lovelies had now appeared. How would he know, until it was too late? Briggs nudged him again. 'Natalie Percy,' he whispered, pointing to a tall young woman wielding a painted fan and smirking at the audience. Verdun dragged his thoughts away from morbidity and tried to concentrate on the story. Apparently Stephen Harcourt was going to marry Pattie Fisher, on the face of it a somewhat unlikely liaison. 'She's good, isn't she?' Briggs said enthusiastically, and Verdun glanced at him in some alarm; he hoped his painful duty among these people was not going to be made even more difficult by adolescent vapourings on the part of his offsider.

'Three little maids who, all unwary, come from a ladies' seminary, free'd from its genius tutelary...' Verdun struggled with the words. Well, St Chedwyn's ladies' seminary certainly was free of its recent tutelary genius, anyway! *'From three little maids take one away...'* Yes, he *would* have to watch young Briggs. The idiot was lapping it up; the fluttering eyelashes over the fans, the mincing walk, the seductive enticements of tiny waists and pretty hands like pink flowers emerging from virginal white sleeves. He should have come alone.

A stir among the audience brought Nick Verdun's attention back to the stage. A tall, angular figure in deep black, with a positively hag-like makeup, had suddenly appeared, seemingly creating a dramatic crisis. He had to look very closely to see that it was Bella Parkinson as the redoubtable Katisha. There was, he could clearly sense, a certain delicious malice in the air; this was the character which should have been portrayed by the woman whose remains now lay, hopefully at peace, in Mason's chapel.

It was equally clear that for some reason there was an element of resentment, perhaps that anyone should have taken on the role, perhaps that anyone should dare to *try!* He wasn't sure. He only knew that the eyes he could see gleaming in the reflection from the stage had a sharply judicial look about them. Bella Parkinson was on trial.

In the first few moments his heart sank with fellow-feeling. Bella was obviously very nervous. Then, as the chorus sang back at her, she rallied; advancing on Nanki-Poo with arms outstretched, she gave every indication that she would swallow him alive. *'These arms,'* she proclaimed, *'shall thus enfold you!'* And Nanki-Poo, with Dave Shafto cowering inside, was hardly acting when he involuntarily stepped backwards, his face registering shocked surprise.

Why? Verdun stared from one painted face to another on stage, and wondered; the orchestra ploughed on, Jasper conducting by the light over his music stand, head down, but above him, for a fraction of a moment, there was absolute stillness. Narrowing his eyes, Verdun tried to see the action from the point of view of the actors, and all at once he knew: Bella Parkinson was not only Katisha. To the others, she was also Teresa Glencosset.

He used the interval for observation, as surreptitiously as was possible in the cramped space available. He bought himself a small can of lemonade and moved slowly, and he hoped inconspicuously, through the throng. It seemed the performance was going well. 'I remember them doing it five years ago,' a man was saying. 'Not bad, not bad at all!'

'What did you think of Bella Parkinson?' as elderly woman asked her companion. Their eyes met over the white wine.

'To tell the truth,' came the reply, 'if I hadn't known I wouldn't have guessed.'

'Just what I thought,' said the first woman. 'Uncanny, that's what it was.'

After a moment her friend said, thoughtfully, 'Perhaps they should have cancelled...'

It was hot, and he slipped outside to find a breath of unused air. Chester Parkinson was there, moving with short, sharp steps up and down the pavement. He nodded without warmth at Verdun, disappearing inside quickly when a bell announced the start of the second half. Nervous, Verdun thought. Not too sure about his wife's sudden rise to fame. Looks like a man who prefers to keep the reins in his own hands. Afraid of being made a fool of! You wouldn't want to be made a fool of in a small town like this.

Briggs was already in his seat when Verdun returned to the stuffy theatre. He himself had seen enough to know that Gilbert and Sullivan hadn't written their operas for him! But he was intrigued. It must mean a great deal to a whole lot of people to make them go on under the circumstances. He let the music flow past him, giving up the attempt to follow the plot, and allowed his mind to find its own level. Tomorrow, whatever pleas were presented to hinder him, the people on that platform must begin to open up. Someone knew the truth.

A kind of musical frenzy indicated even to a philistine like Nick Verdun that the end was nigh. It was a mystery to him where they found their energy. The vicar and Michael Kowalski (the latter resplendent in massive robes that made him look even larger than he was) and a small man the programme named as Pish-Tush (where the hell did they find the names?) were singing fit to bust, and Katisha had her hands squarely planted on Koko's neat shoulders in a proprietorial manner that was probably not doing her husband's nerves any good. Yum-Yum (he groaned again) and Nanki-Poo, it seemed, could go ahead and get spliced, and everything had ended happily, as one could have predicted from the start, thus saving everybody much time and effort. He grinned at his own sour mood, and was misinterpreted by Briggs who said, with schoolboy enthusiasm, 'She was great, wasn't she?'

'Bella Parkinson? Yes, she didn't do badly.'

'Not *her*,' Briggs said, youthfully scornful. 'Natalie Percy! Pitti-Sing. She was great!'

Verdun turned on the boy his most potently acidulous expression; and Briggs, well-versed by now in the incomprehensible behaviour of senior officers, dropped back and allowed himself to consider the possibilities of getting to know Natalie Percy better.

As if his thoughts penetrated the detective's back, Verdun turned. 'No fraternising,' he ordered. 'Back to the hotel now. Bed! Breakfast at seven. Be there! We have a mountain to dig…'

10

Bella Parkinson accepted a cup of coffee from her husband, and sipped it silently, glancing up at him and trying to gauge his mood. It would have been nice if he had been able to bring himself to congratulate her with some of the warmth shown by her on-stage companions, who had surrounded her after the show with enthusiastic protestations of astonishment at her well-deserved success. But she knew Chester too well to expect eulogies; the fact that he had not actually said anything negative was about as positive as he was able to get.

Knowing him as well as she did, she felt that there was more to his dark brooding than a twinge of—of what? Jealousy? He had worn a distant, touch-me-not expression for a matter of weeks, and sooner or later they would have to have it out, remove the mystery, put his mind at ease.

'Well,' she said brightly, when he had failed to speak to her for several minutes, 'I think I'll get off to bed. It's been a long day.'

For a moment she thought that he was going to say something important; his throat moved as if words were stuck there, fighting to emerge' but then he half-turned towards her, not quite meeting her eyes, and said goodnight. As she went along the passageway to the bedroom Bella sighed; but there in the back of her mind were the merry tunes, the fantastic costumes, the general feeling of *companionship*, which was what she chiefly enjoyed about belonging to the G and S. Unbidden, a morsel of Mikado popped into her head and she sang it to herself as she undressed, her mind on other things, quite missing the aptness of the words.

'*The hour of gladness is dead and gone…*' she hummed gently. '*In silent sadness I live alone…*' It was typical of her nature that she did not relate it to her marriage.

Stephen and Mary Harcourt made their way home and had a quiet, relaxing sherry before going to bed. 'I thought you were ever so good,' Mary said, smiling at her husband. 'It went ever so well.'

Stephen accepted the praise graciously. 'Much helped, I should say, by the excellent costumes. You and Dulcet really surpassed yourselves this time.'

'Well, after all, Mikado is so rewarding. So colourful. A pleasure to dress, really.'

They sat in silence, each wrapped in thought. Mary glanced up to see her husband's brow creased with anxiety. 'You're not worried about it, are you?'

'Mikado? No. No!' He pulled himself together.

'Work, then?'

'Well…' He shook his head. 'Not exactly.'

'Tell me?' She smiled encouragingly. He opened his mouth, then seemed to think better of it.

'Nothing to tell,' he assured her, returning her smile. But she was not convinced. 'Let's get to bed. That detective will be all over us tomorrow.'

'How awful!' Mary said. 'I'd almost forgotten about that.' She collected the glasses and took them into the kitchen. 'Wasn't Bella good?'

Stephen agreed. 'Almost too good.' He hesitated. 'Once or twice—I almost thought it was Glencosset.'

Mary put the head around the door, searching his face thoughtfully. 'Is that what's bothering you? That she was like—Teresa?' And Stephen's expression told her that she was not far from the mark.

At the rectory, Charles Culbert was taking a not-quite-hot shower. He had a sense of euphoria, the kind of sensation that sometimes came when he felt he had delivered a good sermon. He wondered whether there was perhaps an element of blasphemy in equating Gilbert and Sullivan with preaching The Word; but took refuge in the knowledge that, as all good things come from God, his small talent must meet with divine approval.

He had been shaken when Katisha had come on stage. The clothes, of course, were the ones Miss Glencosset had worn at the dress rehearsal; the wig also. Bella Parkinson was a well-built woman, though soft where Miss G had been solid. Even so, he had hardly expected the shock of surprise that ran through him when he saw her. In a moment of worldly wisdom he wondered (always supposing the murderer was indeed involved with the production) whether Katisha's arrival had caused even greater havoc in the villain's heart.

Tomorrow would be Thursday, he reminded himself as he dropped the wet towel and donned striped flannelette pyjamas; the day he normally wrote his sermon. Pooh-Bah, Lord High Everything Else, would have to move out of the way and let him get on with parish duties. And, of course, there would be the detective! His spirits drooped at the thought.

Simon Lee, the keys of the theatre safely lodged on his dressing table with his own key-ring and some loose change, sat up in bed reading. He enjoyed the classic mystery stories, the Agatha Christies and the Sayers, those well-loved figures who seemed to attract murder wherever they went. Frankly, if he had been a policeman on a Lord Peter Wimsey case he would have arrested the noble lord on suspicion of being a serial murderer! It was impossible to believe that one man could so frequently have innocent experience of the violent deaths of others.

Then he remembered Nick Verdun, now presumably asleep at the Imperial Hotel. What must it be like to go into a community and sniff around, ferreting out people's private shames, their hidden sorrows, and then present the case in court for the world to sneer at? He put his book away, suddenly losing interest in the literary pursuit of crime. Tomorrow there would be some hard decisions to be made. Detective-Sergeant Verdun was flesh and blood, and he had a sharp eye. As Lee slid down under the bedclothes he shivered suddenly.

Maggie Spenlow removed her mascara in front of the dressing table mirror and glanced through the glass at Jasper, who was standing with a sock in his hand, staring down at it as if it were alive, something disgusting. She had allowed him to come to her bed tonight; it had seemed a fitting way to celebrate a joint success.

'Pleased with Bella?' she said, quite amiable in her relaxed mood.

'Surprised. But pleased, too.' He unfolded his pyjama jacket absently. Somehow, Maggie felt, he was not reacting to her invitation with quite the vigour she had hoped for.

'Something worrying you?'

'No. Why?' He shot a quick glance at her.

'Cat got your tongue?'

For a moment he seemed about to answer, then he shook his head. He picked up the sock and placed it carefully on the top of the jacket, folding them both over his arm like a waiter's cloth. Then he turned towards her, and his eyes were blank, unfocussed, not filled with the delighted anticipation she felt they should be showing.

'I think I'll sleep in the other room,' he said without displaying emotion. 'I'm tired.' And before she could remonstrate with him he had gone, shutting the door carefully behind him. Maggie swung round on her dressing stool. At the far end of the house the door of the 'den' closed firmly.

In his bedroom at the Imperial Nick Verdun closed his eyes and waited while a host of gaudily dressed Japanese used his brain as a stage. Slowly, as he slipped away from reality, the figures changed, becoming slightly sinister, their grotesque faces leering at him, their outrageous costumes a whirl of colour. Suddenly the dagger was there, its hilt cunningly engraved, its tip dripping with blood. Behind it a face reared up, and in a moment of sheer fright he sat up, gasping. Light shone into his room from down the street, where someone had invested in a flashing neon sign; he pulled the thin curtains across and got back into bed.

Who had wielded that dagger? Was it someone he had already spoken with? He turned over on to his other side, and allowed himself to slide away into sleep, the question unanswered.

Two doors away, young Briggs wondered if he would be in town long enough to get something going with the Percy girl.

Over breakfast, Nick Verdun and young Briggs talked about the case. 'It hardly seems as if one of them could have done it,' the youngster said. 'All such good friends and all.'

'You'll find that nothing is impossible in murder cases. Human passions run very deep. And what might seem a good reason to you for murdering someone probably wouldn't affect me that way at all. People have their weak spots,' he said, taking the opportunity to widen his companion's mind. 'Hit them on a strong spot and it has no effect. But hit 'em on a weak one, and it's impossible to tell what the outcome will be.'

'She wasn't popular,' Briggs said. 'Old Glencosset. But that's not a good enough reason for killing her. I can think of a good few...'

Verdun quashed his reminiscent mood. 'She was deep. Seems to have been a highly intelligent, gifted woman. But deep. Devious. Maybe she stood on someone's toes...'

'What are you going to do today?' Briggs asked, as his mentor seemed to have fallen into a thoughtful trance. 'What do you want me to do?'

'Did you find any past form on any of them?'

'No. I rang, like you said. But there are no records in town. Unless they're from interstate—or overseas.'

'I didn't expect it. But it might have helped.' He dropped his napkin on the table and stood up. 'I've got that list from Simon Lee of everyone involved in the production. You can check out all their alibis. Just find out if it can be confirmed where they were from the end of the dress rehearsal until, say, midnight.'

'I thought you reckoned it happened straight after.'

'I think it did. But let's not sell ourselves short. I'm going back to the school now, so you can drop me off.'

The headmistress's study was just being dusted when he arrived. The maid gave him a nervous nod as he entered and then hurried away. He was used to that kind of thing. No one wanted to get too close to a detective. He went straight to the diaries and took out a couple, settling himself at the desk with his pad of paper and preparing to take notes.

When he leaned back an hour or so later he knew that he had been right when he had perused them on that first occasion. Miss Teresa Glencosset had been a dangerous woman. Although much of what she had written was couched in vague and mildly malicious terms, there was enough., if she had told the truth, to lift the lid off much that was going on in the town. Rarely did she use names, and when she did it was usually to tell some unimportant story or relate an inconsequential fact. She scattered her books with initials, which was probably all very well if you knew the people concerned, but meant a heap of deciphering if you didn't. Verdun took an example from the previous year and read it out to himself.

'*If RW had the faintest idea how much I remember and how much there is against him, he would not sleep at nights!*'

And, later: '*That silly cow YE thinks no one see what she does. I have enough to send her away for a lifetime.*'

The final item in the diary for the previous year said, with spiteful jollity, '*Ring out the old, ring in the new! What will the New Year bring? The same old crop of weak, silly people. The same petty criminals. But I have my eye on them, and they shall not get away with it!*'

'Melodramatic nonsense!' Verdun muttered. Someone had brought him a cup of coffee and he hadn't even noticed. He drank it down; it was cold. The diaries alarmed him. Not just because they were obviously full of animosity, but because there was such an air of enjoyment expressed in the brief entries. This had been a nasty, vindictive woman; it sounded like blackmail and, perhaps, if it were, his job would be made easier. There might well be better evidence if money had changed hands at any time.

He closed the books and sat back in the chair, wondering what the headmistress's next step would have been, once she had pinned her specimen down in the diary. Power—was that her game? Just to let people know that *she* knew, too? Just to keep them on the hop, wondering when the truth would be let out? It made a kind of ugly sense.

He wondered where she got her information. This well-appointed study gave one a sense of isolation, of detachment from the world outside. Maybe he should look for an accomplice, though that seemed unlikely. The power-hungry usually preferred to keep their power to themselves.

When Briggs called for him just before lunchtime, Verdun was silent, deep in thought. The youngster drove into town without speaking; he was beginning to recognise the moments when interruptions would be met with heavy sarcasm. He nipped into a deli and bought sandwiches and cool drinks without being prompted; and when he returned to the car his boss was in a more amiable mood.

'What's for this afternoon, then chief?' Briggs enquired cheerily. Verdun grimed.

'What was it the gentleman said? *"I've got a little list"*! And I'm going to work through it. Foot-work, Briggs! Up and down the main street…'

'Pop goes the weasel!' said the constable.

'Oh, very funny!' said Nick Verdun.

11

The collection of data, of getting to know the protagonists in the drama being played out, not on the theatre stage in costume, but among the people who lived and worked in the town, was a time-consuming affair. Verdun's notebook grew fat with detail, dog-eared with constant reference to knowledge gained; and a picture began to emerge of the sub-structure of the community, that part where not much was seen by the passer-by, but was life-blood to the inhabitants.

Sylvia Milton had cleverly fielded a number of phone calls from the irascible client, without ever discovering who he was. She was determined that her boss should not be disturbed during the week of play-acting.

Stephen Harcourt did not know (would not have been particularly interested anyway) that she had tickets for every night of the season; that she sat enchanted as Koko held the stage. She thought he sang 'Tit-willow' with tragic charm, and was glad that she hadn't been able to persuade any of her friends to come with her. This was something she wanted to savour on her own.

When the door suddenly burst open and a large and clearly angry farmer stood glaring at her, she was for a moment nonplussed. He was not, she was sure, a client. The man, in his fifties with the faded blue eyes of one who has gazed at the far horizons, approached her reception desk with the light of battle clearly burning. 'Where is he?' he demanded without preliminaries.

'Where is whom?' Sylvia asked, at her most imperious.

'Your bastard boss! The one who never answers my phone calls. The one who's trying to put me out of business!'

'Are you referring,' Sylvia said in the tones of a dripping icicle, 'to Mr Harcourt?'

'Mr Bloody Harcourt! That's right, sweetheart. The bloke with the mind of a rattlesnake. Is this his office?' He moved towards Stephen's door.

'You can't go in!' Sylvia said, leaping to her feet and somehow managing to place herself between the visitor and the door. 'Without an appointment you cannot enter!'

'And who's going to stop me, sweetheart?'

Sylvia's head went back and she glared furiously at him down her nose. 'I shall!'

'You and whose army?' The man put out an arm to shove her aside, and she, without even thinking, let fly with her foot and caught him on the shin. He gave a bellow of anger.

'You too, eh? Kick a fellow when he's down? Get out of my way, sister, and let me get at him.'

The noise had brought Stephen to his door, which opened just as the farmer was about to slam his hand against it. 'What the devil, Sylvia…?' he began; but the farmer, losing his balance, fell against him and they both travelled at speed across the room and ended against a rank of filing cabinets.

Sylvia, her hands to her face, cried, 'Oh, I'm sorry, Mr Harcourt! I couldn't…' And then, as the men scrambled to their feet and faced each other, glowering, 'Shall I call the police?'

Stephen made a wide, angry gesture that seemed to reject the idea, and closed the door against her anxious gaze. Her failure to protect her boss was so disturbing that she found it necessary to pull out her powder compact and make repairs to her face. Beyond the closed doors she could hear voices raised; but, infuriatingly, no words came through.

'What,' Stephen was now saying with dangerous calm, 'can I do for you?'

'D'you know me?' demanded the stranger.

'I do not.'

'Well, that's mighty odd. Because you're destroying me. And I reckon if you destroy someone you ought at least to recognise them.'

'Sit down,' Stephen said, sitting in his own chair behind the desk.

'I'm damned if I will!'

'*Sit down!*' Stephen bellowed; and the man, taken aback, sat. 'Now,' said Stephen in more reasonable tones, 'we can talk.'

'I haven't come to talk,' said the irate man. 'I've come to knock your bloody block off.'

For a long moment they stared at each other. Then Stephen frowned slightly. 'It's Mr Hailey, isn't it?'

'It is! Perhaps you'd like to tell me why you haven't answered my phone calls.'

'Ah,' said Stephen. 'I overheard… The abusive ones. For a good reason, Mr Hailey. I don't think you left your name.'

The farmer's eyes flashed. 'I thought she'd have known. Or have you got angry clients phoning you all day long? Wouldn't surprise me.'

'Mr Hailey, why don't we talk quietly? Let's get this matter solved. What's your problem?' He injected a soothing, matey note into his voice.

'What's my problem? What's my problem?' Hailey seemed to be about to burst into tears. 'My problem, Mr Harcourt, Developer, is that you are driving me out of existence. That's my problem.'

'Shangri-La?' Stephen said. 'Why does that affect you?'

'Because you've bought up my neighbours on each side, that's why. On one side,' he leaned forward to the desk, drawing with a finger on its surface a large rectangle, 'Bill Capper has sold out.

And here, Willy Johansen has sold out. And here is the main road. And here is scrubland that's impossible to cultivate. And here!' He banged his hand down on the rectangle. 'Here is my land, about to be resumed—*resumed*—by the local shire, so that more bastards can make more money and turn more farmers off the land they and their fathers before them have cared for.'

'You'll be compensated, Mr Hailey. What are you worrying about?'

'I don't want to be bloody compensated!' the farmer roared. 'I want to farm my bloody land!'

'And you think this is all my fault?'

'You're the developer, aren't you? You arranged all this behind my back, didn't you? And you're going to make a packet out of it—aren't you?'

'Development is my business,' Stephen replied, now more at ease.

Hailey leaned back in this chair, hands on knees, directing a look that should have killed. 'Yes, we've heard of your business,' he said meaningfully. 'You and your connections with the shire, You and your connections with the big boys. Well, let me tell you, Mr Harcourt, Developer, there's more than one way of skinning a cat. And there's more than one way of making sure that you and your kind don't prosper. And I'm the bloke to see it gets done.'

He stormed out of the office, past Sylvia, whose eyes shot back to see Stephen sitting brooding at his desk; full of remorse, she hastened to make amends.

'It's not your fault, Sylvia,' Stephen said, a mite wearily for her devotion was not always easy to take; 'it's nothing at all to do with you. Though,' he added, frowning, 'perhaps it would be better if you told me about abusive calls, instead of letting me overhear them…'

As she left, closing the door with almost her normal air of decorum (though her heart was bleeding slightly as she wondered if she had harmed him more by ignoring the abuse), Stephen felt his heart thudding. It had been an ugly encounter. The threats might well be meant. He would have to move carefully. Too many people seemed to want a pound of his flesh.

In spite of the confrontation ('and I should have expected something of the sort,' Stephen reproached himself) it was quite a surprise when, just before closing time, a truck-load of very potent manure was tipped outside his office front door. He didn't bother trying to get the number of the truck, or see the driver; he had no doubt whence the unsolicited gift had come. Sylvia, lips tight and handkerchief to nose, alarmed herself and Stephen by bursting into tears. It had been one of those days.

Michael Kowalski, jovially dividing a side of beef into its component parts, whistled a tune. It was, naturally enough, from Mikado, but that was of no consequence. He was planning how he might best win the delectable Molly de Vance, perhaps even carry her off in romantic style to some butcher's shop in the city. He realised that she was a little older than he, maybe even five years, but he was a mature twenty-seven, and ripe for marriage. Molly would bring glamour into a life that had so far been short of that commodity.

He thought he might wait until the last night of the run, and after the usual winding-down party he would somehow persuade her to let him see her home; optimistic to his back teeth, he was sure that if he presented the case properly she would be unable to resist.

As far as he knew, there was no opposition. Molly was a bit of a flirt, sure, but once she had a husband to devote her seductive ways to she would get over that. He didn't mind seeing that other blokes fancied her—it made the conquest that much more exciting. Saturday night it was, then! He lifted his cleaver and with professional enthusiasm split the carcase down the backbone.

The performances came and went, and Verdun was about his business from early morning. The town became used to seeing him, in the car with Briggs driving, or walking briskly down the main street. If they saw him enter someone's shop or the front gate of a house, work would stop for a moment while possibilities were discussed; local characters were 'volunteered' for the role of murderer, sometimes with an unholy joy, sometimes with mystic awe. It was a moot point whether the community would be pleased or sorry, in general, when the investigation was over and the miscreant safely put away.

Meanwhile, Nick Verdun's list of 'possibilities' had grown to fill several pages, with as many details as could be discovered by an outsider who was treading carefully. He had grown a sensitivity about the place; somehow he felt that this was not quite the same as looking for a city criminal, that the close-meshed spirit of the town would suffer considerable devastation once the result of his researches was known. He wanted to be entirely certain before coming to any conclusion.

One thing still puzzling him was the quantity and variety of information in the dead woman's diaries. It seemed to him that being a headmistress was a fairly solitary thing, that one could hardly join in the common gossip and retain the respect of the parents and students. Yet much of what he read sounded like common gossip; and there was one set of initials that cropped up again and again in relation to these snippets so faithfully recorded day by day. There was someone whose position in the town made it easy to glean information and then pass it on. Him? Her? He leaned towards the latter, simply because it seemed less likely that a man would run to convey the innermost secrets of the township to the daunting Glencosset. The pattern was wrong, though he realised that, with the rising strength of the women's lib movement, this would be seen as a very sexist concept.

So was it for gain, plain old blackmail? Was it for power? Was it a hobby or a source of income? What kind of woman had Glencosset really been? He had yet to hear anyone say a good word—rather, people seemed to shy away from talking about her, though that might have been because she had been murdered. It might be simple embarrassment of the 'don't speak ill of the dead' kind. Whatever it was, it didn't make it any easier for him.

Verdun thought back to the diaries again. He was sure the answer lay in there somewhere.

'How are we doing?' Briggs asked at dinner in the hotel.

'It's a spade job. Lots of digging, and I don't see any real suspect as yet.'

'They're a cagey lot. Do you think *they* know who did it?'

'The G and S crowd, you mean? No—I don't think so. And I can't yet find a motive. So I can't get much further forward. There has to be a reason, after all.'

'Well,' said Briggs reasonably, 'blackmail, anger, money, *crime passionel*,' (he brought this out in what he clearly hoped was a Maurice Chevalier accent), 'though that's a bit hard to believe in the circumstances.'

'Misdirected love can be found anywhere,' Verdun said profoundly.

'Well, no one seems to be pining for her.'

'True enough.'

'Insanity? Mistaken identity? What else is there?'

'I think I fancy the first one,' Verdun said slowly. 'Blackmail. But I've got nothing to base it on except those wretched diaries. She had an extraordinary interest in everyone's goings-on. Why? What did she hope to gain from it?'

They ate their steak and chips in silence. Suddenly Briggs waved his fork.

'Perhaps it's someone who has a thing about Katisha?'

Verdun stared at him morosely. 'Do me a favour! Let's at least keep it in the realms of possibility.' He pushed his plate away. 'If that was so, Bella Parkinson would be in danger.'

'We don't know she isn't,' Briggs said with reason. He shrugged at the look in his superior's eyes. 'No stone unturned!' he said, grinning.

In the foyer of the hotel they separated, Verdun to go through his notes yet again, Briggs to attend his third Mikado in three nights. At the door he turned back. 'Perhaps it was to get La Parkinson into the role?' he said in a penetrating whisper, grinning again as Verdun made a rude gesture and went towards the stairs.

'How would you like to be drummed out of the force?' With a foot on the first step he looked round at the youngster. 'And leave that girl alone!'

Briggs didn't need to ask which one. He had his strategy planned. Natalie Percy would have no defence against the devastating charm he would unleash on her as soon as the performances were done with. He strode along the street to the theatre.

'What, you again?' the woman in the box office said. 'Got your eye on a suspect, have you?'

He flashed a wide smile at her. 'Not exactly a suspect. More of a project!' He entered the gloom of auditorium, the smile still on his face.

Pirt, backstage, standing on guard (against he knew not what) for the third night, watched with fascination as the cast dismantled itself and returned to contemporary Australia. The stage curtains were closed, making an area eminently suitable for a party. The auditorium, which had so recently reverberated to the zestful tum-te-tum of Sullivan's music and the witty tongue-twisting of Gilbert's words, now lay silent and empty, its floors littered with lolly-papers and the odd dropped programme. But behind the all-concealing velvet, trestle tables were being set up; cartons of beer arrived from some hidden store, gin and whisky stood together in a protective group, wine casks appeared out of car boots, little plastic wine-glasses were lined up in serried ranks reminiscent of the mighty troops of Titipu. It was the traditional end-of-run party.

The ladies, bless 'em, had managed among their other duties to 'bring a plate', quiches and lemon meringue pies and chicken wings and remarkably squashy iced cakes, and enough tastefully cut sandwiches to supply a lunch stall. The men, not to be outdone in industry, began to eat them. But Simon Lee tapped his plastic spoon on his plastic glass and called for order.

'It is right that we should celebrate a very successful run of our old favourite, Mikado. But we should also remember for a moment that one of our number is no longer with us.' The party mood took a dive. Faces grew long. Eyes were discreetly lowered. It was suddenly remembered that there was a funeral to attend in a couple of days. 'I don't wish to spoil the evening,' Lee went on, having spoilt it. 'But it would be wrong not to make mention of the tragedy. We should think for a moment of Miss Teresa Glencosset, our leading contralto through a number of seasons, so evilly struck down—and thank Bella Parkinson for having so admirably stood in at such short notice.'

In a burst of enthusiasm engendered as much by relief as by Bella's courageous debut, the party regained its balance, and applauded like mad. Bella, restored to her normal complacent reserve by the removal of her costume, smiled shyly and said it was a great pleasure to have been able to help them out.

'More than helped,' Maggie said, stepping forward and putting her arms around her. 'Played the part as to the manner born.' Jasper nodded, leading another round of applause. Chester, feeling left out, did not clap.

Michael Kowalski edged his way around the crowd to where Molly de Vance was standing. It had not escaped him that she had been ogling a male member of the chorus. He poured a glass of white wine and offered it to her, winking in what he hoped was an intimate, even wicked, manner.

Molly looked up at him under long false eyelashes which she had not bothered to take off. 'I prefer rosé, thanks all the same.' Kowalski, seeing it as a challenge, ruptured another cask to oblige the lady.

For Culbert, who was not your die-hard party-goer at the best of times, this was not the best of times. He had thought he might, in a casual sort of way, offer to escort Molly home through the darkened streets; but, as always, he was too late. Kowalski, young, sturdy, probably virile, outmatched him at every turn. He accepted a glass of beer, feeling very daring, and found himself chatting (with some difficulty, for the noise was now deafening) to an elderly lady recently co-opted into the chorus. It wasn't what he had envisaged as the end to his evening.

Constable Pirt, with a couple of cans of beer in his pocket, felt that his duties were now over and made his way home to Mrs Pirt. Mary and Stephen Harcourt, joining in the revelry, went round the table in opposite directions and were grabbed by animated friends. Dave Shafto, standing in a corner with his back to the jollity, had Pattie Fisher at his mercy and was making social arrangements for what remained of the weekend.

'No, stop messing about, Pat,' he was saying. 'I've kept on asking you—give a bloke a break.'

'Well—all right,' said Pattie, feeling that this was the psychological moment to concede victory. 'Tomorrow afternoon. But don't bring that bike.'

'What's the matter with my bike?' he said aggressively, and she told him to such good effect that on the following day he walked to her house and wandered with her along the winding banks of the little creek at the far end of the town. And actually enjoyed it more than he had expected. (Though mentally apologising to his trusty steed for his perfidious behaviour).

As midnight approached, Bingo Rafferty arrived in a happy state of partial inebriation, and locked himself on to Dulcet Merridew, insisting on telling her a long and involved story about his days in the bush, the end of which he found he could not recall.

'Bingo, dear,' said Dulcet, 'I do think you ought to go home and have a nice sleep.'

'No!' He took her slender arm in his thick hand. 'No! I can't go home.'

'Why ever not, Bingo dear?'

Bingo glanced around him in a surreptitious way. 'Because,' he said in a low rumble into her left ear, 'there's times when a man shouldn't be alone. You understand, Dulce? There's times when a man needs somebody to see him through the night...'

Dulcet regarded him with wide, untroubled eyes. 'Bingo, dear,' she said in clear tones that fell suddenly into one of those silences usually blamed on angels passing o'er. 'I'm not going to sleep with you, if that's what you mean. Certainly not!'

All heads turned their way, and for a moment the silence held. Then someone giggled and someone else clapped, and the meeting broke up in disorder. 'Good on yer, Dulcet!' someone shouted, and someone else yelled 'Good on yer, Bingo!' And Dulcet, not at all put out, said, 'There you are, Bingo! It's not good idea at all.'

Bingo, swivelling his head slowly as if in pain (which, if he imbibed any more, he soon would be), stared around him lugubriously. Dulcet patted his arm as if he were a small child and she his teacher. 'But good try, Bingo!'

Molly allowed Kowalski to escort her from the stage; she had a way of cuddling herself into her coat that he found particularly enticing, and he took her arm and passed through the stage door with her, while his heart thumped a merry madrigal all its own. Once outside, he let the arm slide around her shoulders, and then, slowly and very carefully—for he was not sure of its reception— down to her waist. For a moment Molly considered whether she should put a stop to it at once, or give him a little rope; and then, in flash of time as it so often happened to her, she knew that tonight was to be Mike's night—the unexpected tingling of her flesh, all over her body, told her so in no uncertain manner. Instead of rejecting him, she let herself be pulled within the curve of his arm; and he, sensing the submissive act, responded.

But when he stopped just outside the range of a street light and tried to draw her closer, she held back. 'Not here, silly boy! Someone might see.'

Michael could be heard to murmur that he didn't give a damn who saw, but she put a tiny taloned finger across his lips, taking his hand and leading him away into the dark of a side street. 'Where are we going?' Kowalski asked, bemused by the sudden turn of events.

'To my place, silly,' Molly whispered. 'Isn't that what you want?'

To admit to her that he had never anticipated achieving such sublime heights would be foolish; even in his passionate confusion he could see that. There were tales told about Molly's place—about the things that went on there. But they had never gone further than being rumours; now he would find out for himself. For a moment he shivered, not entirely with excitement: what if he couldn't carry it off? What if…? He took a deep breath. Faint heart, he reminded himself, never won fair lady. And at this moment, under a fragment of moon that lit the planes of her small face, Molly did indeed look fair.

Her cottage backed on to bush, and the front overlooked a narrow lane that was more mud than metal. An old-fashioned archway over the gate hardly seemed Molly's style; but he followed her through it, ducking his head to avoid a long and thorny tendril, and waited impatiently while she unlocked the door. Once they were inside, she closed the door behind him; his heart was thundering fit to burst as he put his hand out, searching for her in the dark.

'Molly! Molly, where are you?' And then, as without warning she slid into his embrace and reached up for his lips: 'oh, Molly…!'

Oh, this was living, he rhapsodised later as they lay together in Molly's bed. *This was what had been missing from his life! This was what a man and a woman were all about. This…!* 'Do shut up,' Molly said from somewhere under his chin. 'What do you want to talk for at a time like this?'

Well, he thought briefly as he let the world slip away from him, she certainly knows what she's doing…! But that would not worry him for several hours yet. Just now it was all he could do to cope with a Molly he had never imagined—a Molly whose true sphere of activity was clearly her boudoir.

By morning, when a clear dawn light showed him a bedroom full of frills and feminine fancies such as he had never occupied before, he was exhausted; he could have slept for a fortnight if she'd let him. But Molly, revealing a nightgown of Hollywood-inspired splendour but also a number of facial wrinkles he had previously failed to notice, flung back the bedclothes and made it clear that it was time to leave.

'Out you go, lover-boy!' she said in tones quite unlike the seductive timbres of the night-time. 'Don't want to get caught with your pants down by the neighbours, do you?'

'But it's Sunday morning, Molly,' he protested.

'Out!' she said mercilessly. 'Through the back door and up through the bush to the top track. Then you won't be seen leaving.'

Half-dressed, feeling more than a little foolish, he turned towards her. 'When can I see you again?'

'Ready for more?' She laughed, and he realised that Molly's laugh was like crystal, sharp, musical enough, but without emotion. 'I'll let you know. In the shop. OK?'

It had to do. She was adamant. She held the trump card, the whip hand. She was the boss! Mike felt a sense of acute frustration sweep through him, but she was not open to argument. He looked back at her as she lay on the frilly pillows, lighting a cigarette and regarding him with ironic amusement.

'It didn't mean anything to you, did it?' he complained, sounding (and knowing he sounded) like a sulky boy.

'Go on with you,' Molly retorted. 'It was good fun, wasn't it?

He wandered slowly up the hill behind the cottage, stubbornly not caring whether he was seen or not. His nerves were jangling, his eyes closed with tiredness, and he had never felt so helpless. As he pounded heavily down the track he decided that he would see no more of her. He would learn his lesson. Molly was strong meat—too strong for him. There had been a girl once before, but it had been nothing like this; with Molly it had been a headlong rush down a mountain side into a lake of ice, and then out again, across burning deserts, through green forests, up to the moon, down into the depths of the earth. He wasn't at all sure he could cope with that too often.

Yet by the time he arrived home and closed the door behind him he knew bleakly that if she beckoned he would come running; and that what he felt for her (even in his torment he knew it wasn't really love) would have to be tested, again and again, until it made him or broke him. He lay down on his bed—his narrow, uncomfortable, male bed—and fell asleep in the middle of a groan.

In her cottage, soaking in a nice hot bath, Molly de Vance smiled secretively and remembered the bits of the night that had pleased her most. He would do, for a while. Until something better came along.

In the rectory, the Rev Charles Culbert made himself a very early cup of tea and wondered how to get through this long Sunday. He was beginning to see that 'the sins of the flesh', which he had always preached on as if they comprised one big package deal, could be separated down into many, many different component parts; and he was sadly afraid that he was coming to know about them in an all too personal way.

Bella Parkinson found Chester standing by the window when she awoke around six on this first Sunday for weeks in which they had been able to relax.

'Can't you sleep, dear?' She herself had slept splendidly, the stresses and successes of the past week combining to make her healthily tired and very satisfied with life. Bur Chester, she realised, had been looking peaky, and perhaps it had not been because of her sudden rise to fame. For here he was, thin-faced and drawn about the eyes, and clearly not happy. 'What is it, Chester?'

'Go to sleep, Bella. I didn't mean to disturb you.'

'But I'm not tired. Let me make you a cup of tea.' She put one leg out of bed.

'I don't want a cup of tea,' her husband answered petulantly. 'Go to sleep!'

'I can't. I think I'll have a cup. Would you prefer coffee?'

'I don't want anything.'

She regarded him thoughtfully. It was obviously going to be one of those days when a wife must use all her skills to avoid a confrontation. A pity, coming so soon on top of her own recent achievements. But she had often noticed that if she had a good day he was sour-tempered. Just one of those things, she told herself without rancour, slipping on her dressing gown. Just one of the little hiccups in married life. She would make him a cup of tea anyway, and he would probably enjoy it.

Back in bed, balancing the cup carefully on her knee, she watched Chester as he went noisily into the bathroom and had a shower, then returned to stump around the bedroom, searching for things that were all the time under his nose, being as irritating as a man can be in such a mood. 'Drink your tea,' she said gently, and he took a sip.

'It's cold.'

'I'll pop it in the microwave...'

'Don't bother.' He took out a pile of handkerchiefs, spilling them on the bed irritably.

'What are you looking for, dear?'

'The blue one with the stripy border.'

'It's in the wash. Won't another one do?'

He sat down heavily on the side of the bed. 'I *wanted* that one,' he said, as a child might say about a puppy in the pet shop window. Bella sighed. This was not really how she had hoped to spend Sunday.

By lunchtime even Bella's patience was wearing very thin. As they drank coffee in the little sunroom they had built out at the back of the shop accommodation, she tried again. 'What are you worried about, Chester dear?'

His reaction did not surprise her. 'Worried? Who says I'm worried?'

'*I* say you're worried,' she said, leaning forward and touching his hand. 'You're like a bear with a sore head. You haven't said one nice thing to me all day.'

'What did you want me to say, then?' he demanded belligerently. 'Something nice about last night, I suppose?'

'It would have been—kind, dear. I value your opinion above all others, as you know.' She smiled to show she wasn't too hurt. Chester, looking a little ashamed of himself, half turned towards her.

'You did well. I said that before. And they all seemed pleased with you. What more can I say?'

'I thought perhaps you were angry.'

'Angry? What about?'

'Because I was—well, because they'd asked me…'

'Oh, good God!' He flung his arms out, ridiculously dramatic. 'Why should I worry? Why should I be angry? If they think you're good enough…'

'So if they ask me again next year…?' She felt as if she walked on egg-shells.

He exploded. 'Do what you damn well like! I probably shan't even be here.'

There was a mighty silence between them. Bella stared at her husband and he stared at a plant in the window. At length she said, 'What do you mean?'

Chester stood slowly, looking, she thought, quite like an old man. 'I mean that…that I've…'

'Are you in some kind of trouble, Chester?' She put her cup aside and slipped out of the chair, going to her husband and putting a hand on his back. There was a long moment before he nodded, his head hanging, all the bombast suddenly gone. 'What…?'

But suddenly she could not ask any more; for the remembrance of what had happened in the theatre dressing room came to her, and she dared not put into words what she feared. Chester? Chester couldn't do *that*, not even to that dreadful woman Teresa Glencosset. Chester was often difficult, frequently hurt her feelings with his pedantic coolness; but he couldn't do *that*! 'Oh, my dear!' she said, and rested her head against his shoulder.

'I knew while I was doing it that it was stupid,' he said in a low, weary voice. Chester admitting to being stupid? She closed her eyes. 'It wouldn't solve anything. It would only make things worse than they already were. But things were piling up, and I couldn't see a way out. And I couldn't bear to tell you—I didn't want to lose your respect. I was afraid of losing you, Bella...' Suddenly, improbably, her husband was in her arms, crying like a baby. Bella tightened her grasp automatically, but her brain was racing. How would they cope with this? How would they support each other through the days ahead?

'You'll never lose me, Chester.' She was speaking with one part of her brain, saying the things that would comfort. In another part of her head a wild confusion reigned. *Chester*, of all people! Calm, cool, disciplined Chester—the man she had worshipped as a girl, adored as a bride, and submitted to all things as a wife—had cracked at last. And a sudden surge of passionate, maternal love swept her as she cradled his grey head against her. 'I don't care what you've done, my darling. I shall never leave you. I would lie and cheat and starve for you, Chester, you know that. And before he can get to you, Sergeant Verdun has to get past me!'

She was Boadicea; she was an Amazon queen; she was Joan to his Darby. Chester made a strangled noise against her shoulder, and he drew away from her a little, staring at her face in horror.

'What do you think I've done?' he said in a voice shaking with emotion. '*What are you talking about?*'

She smiled proudly. 'A woman's place is beside her man,' she proclaimed in tones borrowed from Katisha. 'Together we shall win!'

'Win what?' He took her arms and shook her a little. 'What do you think I've done?'

She stared at him, suddenly afraid of the look in his eyes. 'I thought...'

'You thought—you thought it was *me* who killed Miss Glencosset? You thought that? You could think that of me, your husband? Get away from me, woman! Look at me—am I a killer? Am I?'

The tears were over. He was angrier than she had ever seen him. But she had to know. 'Then what...?'

'The shop,' he said, his back to her. 'We're broke. It's been going down for months, and now it's finished.'

Bella could find no words. What he was saying seemed to have no meaning. Beside what she had thought he meant, this was nothing. 'I'm so sorry,' she said at last. 'So sorry.'

They sat together in silence, and her mind wandered through the maze his words had opened up. They were broke; well, they would start again. People did. They would be together, even if they had to live in a caravan, on the dole, eating cheap cuts of meat and making-do with old clothes. She could bear it. But what had he meant by being 'stupid'? She could hear his voice as he said it: 'I knew while I was doing it that it was stupid'. *What* was stupid? Going broke? But he hadn't actually 'done' that; rather, it had happened. 'What was it that was stupid?' she asked suddenly. 'What would make things worse?'

He would not meet her eyes. 'I tried everything to save it,' he said finally. 'But it was like pouring water down a drain. Then...'

'Then what?' she said, when he came to a halt. 'What was it you did, Chester?'

'I—used some other money. Just as a loan, to keep things going a little while longer.'

'A loan? I don't understand.'

'I used the G and S money! I wrote cheques as treasurer and paid them to myself—made out to cash.' He groaned. 'I knew it was futile, I knew that when the crash came...But I hoped there wouldn't be a crash. I hoped there'd be a—a miracle of some sort. That trade would turn around and I'd be able to pay it all back without telling anyone.'

She stared at him. 'But, Chester...'

'Oh, I know. Don't start nagging.'

'I'm not nagging. But I have to know.' She felt strength flow into her. The hidden talents that Mikado had brought out would be useful now. 'You have to tell me, dear. You mustn't keep me in the dark, ever again.' She frowned. 'I thought you had to have two signatures on the cheques, yours and Simon's.'

'I asked him to sign some in advance, to save time. And he did it—because her trusted me!' He put his head into his hands. 'I told him there were amounts to settle—and now...'

The disgrace! She shuddered slightly as the knowledge took hold. But her place was with Chester, whatever he had done; and embezzling (she supposed that was what it was) was not as dire as murder. They would survive.

'Thank God it wasn't—the other,' she said quietly, standing up to clear their cups away. Chester glanced up at her.

'You couldn't really think I had done that?' She looked down at him. She was sorry he was in control of himself again; she had rather enjoyed the sensation of holding his weeping body in her arms.

'Someone did,' she said sombrely. 'Someone is going to have to bear the shock when they find out who. I'm glad it isn't me.'

He rubbed his hand over his face. 'Perhaps they won't find out.'

'That would be terrible.'

'Whoever did it,' he said in a voice that made her turn back from the door to look at him, 'was a public benefactor. She was a vile woman!'

Once again Bella felt a tremor of fear run through her. She knew, from the expression on his face, that he hadn't told her everything.

Dave Shafto emerged from behind a dilapidated barn with Pattie Fisher's lipstick all over his face and neck and her promise to let him take her out again next weekend. They'd had a good time together, fish and chips after the walk by the creek, and a long session of panting excitement offering much and achieving little. Pattie's mother was with them in spirit; it seemed that the old lady (mid-forties seemed pretty old to Dave) would find out everything they had done, and Pattie would prefer not to have too much to confess.

But it had been one way of taking his mind off things. He could feel retribution on the way, and he didn't mean Mrs Fisher. He could kick himself for being a fool: it had taken him years of effort to get to be a bank teller, a trusted position in any town, and now everything was hanging in the balance—and he could blame no one but himself.

One thing, he'd cut himself off from Pete and Col; that was all behind him now, and if it came to it he would say so. 'Your Honour,' he would say, 'I'm going straight from now on. I've learnt my lesson.' But the face that lowered over the judge's bench at him in his dreams was hard and suspicious, and his promises sounded like so much hot air.

'Indeed?' his dream judge would reply; 'well, just to make sure, I'll sentence you to two hundred years in prison!'

Waking up, unfortunately, was hardly more reassuring.

Then there was the additional worry: the phone calls. He couldn't imagine how anyone had caught on to what he had done. But the caller had known, somehow. Enough to get the wind up him, to frighten him out of his wits the first time it had happened. And when he realised who…He shivered now, as he made his way home. He was in real trouble. If it all came out…

Young Briggs, feeling that as it was Sunday he could imagine himself off duty, located Natalie Percy as she wandered aimlessly down the street with a couple of friends, and persuaded her to have a cup of coffee with him at the Tudor Tea Shoppe. They found a table just inside the frilly-curtained bay window, and he set out to do a bit of detecting on his own behalf. 'What time do you finish work?'

'Five-thirty. Why?' Natalie regarded him suspiciously. She had never been this near to a policeman before—and certainly not a detective.

'I thought we might—go for a little walk,' he said, wondering what on earth there was to do in this place now that Mikado was finished. 'What do you usually do after work?'

'Go home,' she said forbiddingly. She wasn't yet quite sure if this was an interview or something more friendly. The coffee came, and Briggs sipped at his while he considered his next move.

'So what about a walk?' he said.

Natalie glanced up at him through her lashes, not quite smiling. 'Why?'

Young Briggs, feeling that he was making progress backwards, grinned at her cheerfully. 'I thought we might get to know each other better.'

Natalie stirred her coffee slowly. 'Not much point,' she said at length, 'with you going back to town any day.'

'Well, not until the case is cracked, anyway.'

'Your Sergeant Verdun's a bright one, isn't he? It won't take him long. Little place like this—it's not like your city crime. Not many could've done it.'

Briggs stared at her for a moment. His professional interest momentarily took over his personal desires.

'Who do *you* think...?'

Natalie put up a warning hand. 'Oh, no! I'm not doing your guessing for you. Safer not to.'

'What do you mean, safer?'

'Well, it stands to reason,' she said, not meeting his eye. 'It's a small town. Someone in it has done a murder—we don't know who. But there's lots goes on in a small town, lots of things that a visitor wouldn't see. So the ones that live here have to be pretty careful. After all, when you've done your detecting and gone back to the city—we shall still be here.' She looked across the table at him, and he saw a quick flash of something more than the shy flirtatiousness of a girl with a new man.

'If you know something,' he began, slightly pompous, 'you have to tell us. That's the law...'

'I don't know anything,' she said quickly, with finality. 'And if you asked me here to talk about Miss Glencosset's murder you can think again.'

She drank her coffee down as if she was about to leave. 'No!' Briggs said. 'No, I didn't. I wanted to get to know you—honest. The other just sort of—came up.'

Natalie relaxed, but her eye on him was wary. 'As long as you understand,' she warned him. 'Get your murderer and go! We just want to be left alone.'

After that, the atmosphere warmed slightly; but young Briggs could not rid himself of the idea that she was weighing every word.

It worried the policeman in him, especially because he knew that everything he discovered must go back to Verdun. And that put him in an invidious position with Natalie. He sighed silently, and leaned towards her. 'Tell me about yourself,' he said in what he hoped was an inviting tone of voice; but he was painfully aware that, whatever he said to her, he sounded like a cop.

Jasper and Maggie Spenlow, walking back from the theatre, where they had been clearing away some of the after-show debris, passed the Tudor Tea Shoppe window. 'Look,' said Maggie; 'Natalie with that young policeman. He didn't hang about, did he?'

Jasper glanced through the window. Briggs and the girl had their heads together over the tiny tea-table, engrossed in conversation. He was not pleased by the sight.

'I don't think we should get too involved with the police,' he said shortly.

'We?'

'The people who live here. We should keep them at arm's length. Totally professional.'

'Perhaps he's giving her the third degree. Or something!,' Maggie said with a slightly malicious grin. Jasper wore an expression of distaste.

'I don't think that's funny, Maggie.'

She shrugged, amused. 'Sorry!' Jasper strode ahead of her and she followed; how irritating he could be! What could Natalie possibly know that even young Briggs would be interested in? What did any of them know, come to that?

13

The Rev Charles Culbert stood in the church vestry preparing for the funeral. He was finding the whole business profoundly depressing, and wished with some fervour that he could be somewhere else, let someone else take it. He wondered if he might be going to be ill; the strange sensations he had suffered in these past days had certainly had an odd effect on him. Never a heavy eater, he was finding it difficult even to sit down to a meal; never a drinker, he kept turning towards the cupboard where he kept a bottle of medicinal brandy and a small amount of sherry for visitors. It had even crossed his mind that he ought to go to the bishop and declare himself an unfit person to be shepherd to these lackadaisical sheep who sat, Sunday by Sunday, nodding off in front of him as he delivered sermons intended for their ultimate salvation.

He could hear the shuffling of feet as people entered the church—he wouldn't dignify them as 'mourners', for he much feared that no one in this church today would be mourning Miss Glencosset. And this was part of his problem. Even when dealing with the obsequies of someone he didn't know, he usually found it possible to say a few apposite words, to give dignity and meaning to this ending of a life. There would be a widow, or children, or even a parent who would find some flavour of comfort in his words; but what could he say about Teresa Glencosset? At least, what could he say *and mean it?*

The coffin, he knew, was lying on the bier at the front of the church. The organ was playing softly. It was time. He opened the vestry door and stood for a moment surveying the unusually crowded nave. As he had expected: the place was full. Everybody loves a murder!

A sound as of dry autumn leaves announced that the congregation was rising to its collective feet. Eyes were on him. He took a deep breath. *'I am the resurrection and the life, saith the Lord; he that believeth in me, though he were dead, yet shall he live: and whosoever liveth and believeth in me shall never die...'*

'But *she* died,' Nick Verdun was thinking, at the back of the church. 'Someone wanted her to. Someone took her life before she was ready to go, and that's why I'm here—to see that people don't take decisions into their own hands.' He let his eyes roam across the heads of those who had felt drawn to this macabre occasion.

For a moment he scorned them for their morbid curiosity; then he allowed himself to warm slightly, to see it from their point of view. Of course they were interested when someone was done to death in their community: why not? It was the great mystery. It was *'there but for the grace of God go I'.* It was *'in the midst of life we are in death'.*

He slipped quietly out and drove himself back to the school. Briggs, whose legs were younger, had been sent on an errand.

'We dislike doing this kind of thing,' the bank manager said to young Briggs, reprovingly, as if some of it was his fault.

'I appreciate that,' said Briggs, who had been told to be tactful. 'If Sergeant Verdun didn't believe it was necessary we wouldn't be doing it. We dislike it,' he said virtuously, 'as much as you do. But we do have authority.'

'Then what is it you want to know?' the manager said, sighing. Once he knew, he went to work silently to produce the information Verdun had asked for. Briggs, writing in his notebook, copied down names and figures and, coming to an end, thanked the manager with a cheery smile and made his way out into the street.

In the teller's cubicle, Dave Shafto watched him go, and his stomach churned with fear. Not this time, then; but surely next time, or very soon. He closed his cash drawer and made his way to the toilets. But the sickness he felt was in the mind, and his body, unfeelingly, would not give him the chance of claiming the need to go home where he could close the door and keep the world at bay for a little longer.

Young Briggs, beginning to enjoy himself, called at the next bank along the main street, and then at the third and last. This was detecting! Probing and poking, uncovering and revealing! It beat running in drunks any day.

Verdun, meanwhile, was back in Miss Glencosset's study with the diaries. They fascinated him, at the same time promising great things and yet withholding them. Quite a Nostradamus, the headmistress! A roundabout way of putting things, making her entries incomprehensible to anyone simply opening the books; but for him, with the need to discover the truth, endless frustration.

What was he to make of this, for example? '*How long does RN think he can pull the wool over my eyes? I shall speak to him one day, and he will see that I KNOW ALL!*' Perhaps it was all just dramatic nonsense, created by a lonely woman for her own pleasure. Yet he was sure it was not that easy. Virtually every entry seemed to hold at least the breath of a threat, and some were far more blatant than that. He came back, as always, to the question: where did she get her information?

The same pair of recurring initials were at least one source. On an impulse he called for Mrs Parker, the deputy head, and when she arrived—looking as anxious as most people do when summoned by the police—he asked, 'Did Miss Glencosset have any regular visitors?'

'Well,' said Mrs Parker, her eyes wide with the effort of thinking, 'it would be difficult to say.'

'Someone must know. One of the maids?'

'Daytime, yes. People with appointments would be shown in here. Their names would be in the engagement book. But the domestics go off duty at six, and the headmistress's house, as you see, is not part of the main school building. So if Miss Glencosset wanted to see someone here in the evenings I doubt if anyone would know, except by accident.'

'Seems rather odd, then,' Verdun said, feeling his way, 'that she wasn't killed here.'

'I suppose it is,' Mrs Parker said, unused to such channels of thought.

'I mean, at the theatre it was all go, and it must have been difficult to find her alone for long enough to—to...'

'Whereas here—yes, I see what you mean!' She sounded quite excited. 'In the dark, the house facing the front, very easy to arrive unseen by anyone else—yes, I see what you mean.'

'Ah, well,' Verdun said, relaxing and smiling at her, 'if we could predict the strange workings of the criminal mind we would all sleep a little easier.'

But it *was* odd, he repeated as he made his way back into the town. By killing her in the theatre the murderer virtually limited the number of suspects. He pulled into the hotel forecourt and parked the car. He had all the initials he could garner from the diaries; now he must check them against his lists. If young Briggs had had any luck at the banks they might narrow the field down. It should be an easy case to crack, yet for the moment he felt quite inadequate to do so. He would sit up tonight until he had an answer of some sort; tomorrow, anyway, he must ring in a report to his superior. It would help to hold off that individual's sarcasm if he had a few juicy details to impart.

'Are you all right?' Sylvia Milton had entered her boss's office with a pile of papers to sign and found him staring at the front of the filing cabinets. He turned a weary face to her.

'Quite all right. Why do you ask?'

'You look so tired.' She yearned for him. 'Mr Harcourt—Stephen—if you need someone to talk to, I'm very discreet.'

He looked up, puzzled. 'I'm sure you are, Sylvia. And thank you. If I should ever need to talk...'

'Oh, why try to hide it from me?' she cried, taking both of them by surprise. 'We've worked together for years, Mrs Harcourt—Stephen—and I can see how tired you are, how worried. *Why* won't you share your problems with me? I could help you, I know I could.'

Stephen pulled himself up in his chair, astonished. He had always found Sylvia to be an excellent secretary; she worked competently and seemed as if outside the office she would have no interest in his business dealings. She had never been taken into his confidence about the more 'difficult' jobs, nor was she *au fait* with the wheeling and dealing that inevitably went on when negotiating land sales. Her sudden eruption as an emotional force in the office was alarming, to say the least.

'My dear Sylvia,' he began, floundering a little. 'My dear, there is always something to worry about in this job. The timing has to be just right, the price must be acceptable on both sides, the...'

'It's more than that,' she cried with passion. 'I've watched you these past weeks. There's been something gnawing at you...' She said it with dramatic fire, and he thought, inconsequentially, that perhaps she should join the G and S.

'Gnawing? Oh, come! A few tricky deals, maybe, but nothing...'

'Mr Harcourt! Don't try to pretend with me. I *know*!!'

His eyes narrowed and he stared at her. 'You know what?' he said, his voice level.

'I know that there is something dreadfully wrong. That man who left the—the manure...it's him, isn't it? It's something terrible to do with him?'

Relieved, Stephen Harcourt gave a laugh. 'Nonsense, Sylvia!' He came round the desk and put his hand on her arm. She bit her lip and stood quite rigid, wondering if he could comprehend what the gentle touch was doing to her. 'Mr Hailey is very excitable. He doesn't mean half he says.'

'It didn't look like that from out there.'

'Then you must take my word that it is so.' He patted her kindly. 'Take a couple of hours off, Sylvia. I'll manage until after lunch.'

But she shook her head stubbornly. If she were not there, outside his door, who could tell what threats he might have to endure, what disasters might fall upon him? She couldn't take that risk. 'I shall stay,' she said, her chin rising courageously.

'That's the girl!' Stephen said admiringly; and was doubly astonished when, with a sad little cry of pain, she fell against him and flung an arm around his neck. 'What the hell...?'

But Sylvia could only moan gently in her anguish, and feel, paradoxically, a sense of delicious peace steal over her as her boss's arms enclosed her.

'There. there,' he was saying. 'There. there!' And then, 'Take my hankie, Sylvia. Have a good blow—you'll feel better.'

Back at her desk, Sylvia felt herself blush from head to toe at the dreadful exhibition of her secret admiration; through the office window she could see him as he wrote at his desk, and now and then he looked up and gave her a little nod of encouragement. But far more memorable than her own foolishness was the strong feeling of his arms around her; when she recalled that moment she could actually feel his powerful muscles and smell the manly freshness of his laundered shirt.

Within the office Stephen wondered if he should ask Sylvia to leave. He wanted no complications with love-sick secretaries, especially not at this moment. Then he considered how hard it would be to find another job, and how she had been faithful for so long. He must just take care to see that it could never happen again.

His mind went back to the business with Hailey. And then slid, as it tended to do, to this morning's funeral and the presence of the detectives in town—the whole ghastly mess. He wouldn't be easy until he saw them driving off back into the city, hopefully with a handcuffed suspect in the back of the car—someone, anyone! Meanwhile it was imperative that there should be no rumours that could reach Verdun's ears. He glanced out at Sylvia and gave her another little nod. He could trust her—couldn't he?

The next evening, Tuesday, was traditionally the informal general meeting for the Gilbert and Sullivan Society, when the previous week's performances would be analysed and discussed, and preliminary plans made for the next annual production.

The Green Room was packed, with standing room only (or at best a corner of someone else's chair) for the late-comers. Simon Lee looked round him with some satisfaction; it was a thriving, energetic society, and he was proud of it. He rapped for attention.

Mary Harcourt, G and S secretary, announced in gentle tones that a wreath had been sent to the funeral from the society, and a murmur acknowledged the fact. She mentioned that the annual barbecue for members, families and friends would be held on Saturday at Nicholson Park, everyone bring a plate, and would the treasurer please see that there were ample coins for the gas operated barbies this year, bearing in mind last year's fiasco?

This was followed by a report from the treasurer, Chester Parkinson, and the noise subsided as Chester, his face a peculiar shade of grey, got to his feet.

'He's not looking at all well,' Dulcet Merridew said with real concern in her voice, leaning towards her neighbour, Molly de Vance. 'He doesn't have a heart, does he?'

'Not the way you mean,' Molly said, grinning wickedly. Chester began to speak, his voice strained, his hands shaking with a fine tremor which was new to them.

'This was in some ways our most successful season yet.' He glanced around the group, without actually meeting any eyes. Beside him, Bella sat composedly, watching him. She was willing him to pull through this ordeal. 'Ticket bookings were up by a fifth, and door sales were twice what they were last year. This may well be because it was Mikado. It's popularity never wavers. And…' He cleared his voice nervously. 'And I suppose we must assume that our unfortunate tragedy may have brought in some who would not otherwise have attended. It seems a terrible thing to say—but we all know there are those who are attracted by—by such terrible acts.'

Maggie thought, '*He's having real difficulty in saying "murder".*' Beside her, Jasper was shifting in his chair.

'Damned tactless,' he muttered; but around him heads were nodding.

'I'm afraid that's very true,' Simon Lee said. 'So we have broken even, Mr Treasurer?'

'More than that,' Chester Parkinson said, attempting a smile. 'We have broken our own record, which I believe was "Yeomen", some years ago. Congratulations!'

Amid a spattering of applause he sat down. 'You will let me have the details in due course?' Lee suggested, and Chester nodded, his voice drying into a croak.

Michael Kowalski stared across the room at Molly, trying to catch her eye. He had made great endeavours to get a seat beside her; but she was behaving oddly, it seemed to him, never able to meet him since that night that still made him burn when he thought of it, and refusing to come with him tonight without giving a reason. He knew all about women playing 'hard to get', and he would argue it out with her later. Meanwhile, he needed to establish eye contact with her, and this she was apparently not prepared to allow, chatting instead to Dulcet with every appearance of thorough enjoyment.

There was a strange constraint about the meeting, Maggie Spenlow was thinking, as if much that ought to be said was being withheld. She caught an expression of—what?—sadness, or frustration, or something deeper on the long, thin face of the Rev Charles. She wondered why so many of the men she met who had opted for the church bore that stoically depressed attitude. What would it take to get the man to let go with a real belly laugh? What (in private, when he could let his hair down) would tickle his funny bone? She grinned at the thought, looking at his sparse crowning glory.

The vicar was indeed wondering why he had come. They could do everything that needed to be done without him. No one would ask for a blessing on the meeting, or a prayer for the future of the society. They would probably all be grateful if he got up and went, so that they could drink their beer and tell their risqué stories without inhibition. But when he looked across the room he knew why he was there; it was the only place he could be sure of seeing Molly. And seeing Molly had become a pressing need for him.

He hated himself for his weakness; he almost hated her for the effect she was having on him; and he had the greatest difficulty in not hating Michael Kowalski, who was even now winking across the room, his ruddy cheeks redder than usual, his nonchalant air no disguise for his feelings. Charles Culbert knew all about nonchalant airs these days; maintaining his own equilibrium was a full-time battle, and he knew he was losing the war. He would have to go, leave this safe country retreat that had suddenly turned into a burning Hades of passions and angers and—he suddenly remembered Miss Glencosset, so recently cremated. Somewhere in this small, law-abiding town, perhaps even in this room, was the person who had let venomous hatred suppurate until he or she had resolved the conflict in the act of murder.

He felt a swift rush of blood to his face. What had he, a man of God, to do with such sinfulness? How had he let himself descend so low? He looked across the room to where Kowalski sat, legs splayed wide, stomach proudly displayed in a stretched knitted sweater probably made by his mother. What was he doing, hating that young man? He, who had been taught about the love of God, about forgiveness, about redemption! As Kowalski turned, feeling the reverend eye upon him, Culbert managed a small grimace which the butcher interpreted correctly as a smile, returning it with a cheery nod.

Culbert closed his eyes for a moment and allowed a gentle trickle of warmth to enter his tired soul. These tormenting dreams were not for him.

When he opened his eyes again he found that Molly de Vance was looking across at him, and the spiritual warmth turned to a torrent of passion when, picking her moment with the sure touch of the expert, she half-closed her eyes at him, slowly, cheekily, and he had to admit, sexily. Stumbling to his feet he made his apologies to the president—'urgent business to complete before tomorrow morning'—and hastened from the room.

Molly, watching him go, grinned to herself and wriggled a little inside her silky dress; and Michael Kowalski, mightily encouraged, made the mistake of thinking that she was directing it at him.

By the time Bingo Rafferty arrived the meeting was grinding to a close. The one subject everyone wanted to talk about had tacitly been avoided: the murder, funeral and police investigation. But Bingo had no such finer feelings. After making his apologies in a well-lubricated voice, he forced himself into a small space beside Dulcet Merridew (overlapping her considerably, though she didn't seem to mind), and enquired, 'Police arrested anyone yet?'

Brutal it might be, but it was the one thing needed to get everyone going. Rumour was rife, and neighbours swapped stories with gusto, ranging from the personal observation to the relating of third or fourth hand information. Simon Lee regarded them with some dismay at first; but then, watching the cut-and-thrust, question-and-answer around him, he understood that they needed to talk, to get it all out into the open.

Chester Parkinson, his colour somewhat improved, rose and withdrew with his wife, nodding briefly to Lee. A few minutes later

Maggie and Jasper left, though Maggie looked as if she would like to have stayed and joined in the gossip. By the time the meeting broke up into small groups congregating outside the theatre and in the car-park, the whole police investigation had been taken apart (and found wanting), and some of the heavy burden of suspicion had been lifted from the society. For, after all, how could it have been someone with whom they had spent such a lively evening? How could it be someone well known to them? How could it be...?

It was only as the separated to go home that the understanding began to seep back that, however improbable it might be, *someone* was carrying a very guilty secret.

15

Michael Kowalski had a wager with himself, and to his surprise he won. Molly wandered out of the Green Room as if she had no idea in the world that he was waiting outside for her; and when he took her arm she went with him, meek as a lamb, just as if she hadn't been avoiding him for the past three days.

They walked together, arms entwined, his attention entirely on her, hers on the meeting they had left. He wondered how he should introduce the subject of where they should go, his place or hers, without bringing down in his head her well-known scorn. She was a funny one, was Molly; you could never tell exactly where you were with her, not even when your arm was as far round her waist as it could go. He opened his mouth to speak.

'Odd, wasn't it?' Molly said, before he could get the words out. 'That meeting. As everybody knew something, but no one knew everything. Really weird!' She looked up at him. 'Who did it, Mike? Who do you think?'

He looked down at her seductive mouth and bent to kiss it. 'Who cares?' he began to say.

'No, stop fooling about!' she said, irritation in her voice. 'It's important. Who killed her?' She pulled away a little, staring at him. 'Here, it wasn't you, was it?'

He gazed at her in consternation. "Course it wasn't me!' The mood shivered and fell around him in fragments. 'What made you say that?'

'It was someone,' she said in a low voice. 'Someone did it! Someone we know. So it could've been you.'

His disappointment made him abrupt. 'Or you!' he retorted. 'Why not a woman? Old Glencosset had it in for anyone, she didn't care who.'

They were walking apart by this time; Molly turned to look at him in the silver light from a cloudless, moon-filled sky. 'You, too? What had she got on you?'

Mike shrugged. He should have kept his big mouth shut. 'Nothing. Just a lot o' nonsense.' He must repair the damage this conversation had done to their evening; putting out a tentative arm he found her not unwilling, and drew her to him.

'She was a wicked old bitch,' Molly said suddenly, and he felt her shiver against him. 'It's just as well she's dead.' Then, in one of paradoxical changes that had flummoxed better men that Kowalski, she smiled provocatively up at him. 'What are we talking about her for? Coming to my place, are you?'

Mike had spent many an hour on the football field, running until he felt he would drop, but finding his second wind in time to kick the final goal or outrun his opposition. He believed himself to be fit and full of endurance. But a night with Molly de Vance would have tried the staying power of a Roman gladiator. Towards morning he rolled away from her, exhausted, wanting only a cigarette and a cup of strong coffee.

Molly, on the contrary, was full of energy, and as dawn lightened the room she had a shower and emerged as if she had had the best night's sleep ever.

'Coffee,' she said. 'Here, wake up!' He turned his head, his eyes feeling like sand heaps. 'No stamina, that's your trouble,' she mocked. 'Drink your coffee, then I've got something special for you.'

'What?' He was done for. Sleep, he begged silently.

'Be a good boy and you'll see.'

The little silver box she produced gave him no warning of what it might contain. When she opened it, holding it where he could see it with one bleary eye, he said, 'What is it?' and she grinned knowingly.

'Top quality! Brought it in myself. Going to try some?'

He struggled up and took a better look. What was it? Something white—something powdery! His brain seemed to have stopped working. Something *white* and powdery. For heaven's sake! It was a *white powder!* And he suddenly realised what he was looking at.

'Here—that's whass'name? Cocaine? That's cocaine, that is! Where d'you get it?'

'Ah! That'd be telling. Have a go—go on! You'll love it.'

He sat up in the bed, shaking his head violently. 'Not me! No way—that's a mug's game.'

'That's what they say, love. But I'm OK. Look at me! Never done me any harm.' She wriggled up against him. 'Go on! Be brave! Have a go!'

He could never explain to himself afterwards why he did it. He must have been loony, he cried within himself, as he emerged from an experience worse than any he had ever known. Molly's reaction was quite different; she seemed to be able to accommodate the terrifying swing of mood that had him shouting for help at one moment, fearing death the next. When he recovered enough to dress and go home—to the shop, rather, for it was past the time he usually opened—Molly was lying back against the pillows with a strangely alien look about her. It was difficult to believe that only a few hours ago…he shut off the memory.

'I'm going,' he said. 'Don't ever—ever ask me…'

'What, lover-boy?' she said, smiling a secret smile. 'Don't ever ask you to come back to my place?'

'Don't ever ask me to touch that—that stuff again!'

Molly stretched her toes down to the foot of the bed. 'You're a right softie,' she mocked him. 'A proper old sook! Takes a man to cope with Molly. And there aren't any *men* in this town, are there? Molly'll have to go somewhere else…'

Mike, feeling betrayed and foolish and, now and again, very frightened, stood in the doorway and looked back. 'You'll come to no good, Molly de Vance! You'll kill yourself with that stuff. An' if they find out you bring it back…'

'Who's going to tell them, eh?' She leaned forward, dragging a pillow from behind her and throwing it at him. 'You—you sooky kid? Any of your softie friends? God, how I hate this town.' She gave a strange growl, like an angry cat, and stretched out her hands to him like claws. 'There's no one here good enough for Molly. Get out! Get out, you big soft fool! While you can…'

Kowalski, defeated, unmanned, weary to dropping point, disillusioned almost to tears, left the house and made his way up through the paddock and on to the track. His head felt as if it belonged to someone else, his body ached and burned; but the yearning had gone. Molly in the mood he had just seen was a vixen, a wild-cat, and he would have nothing more to do with her. As he made his shamed way to the shop he felt a reaction rising in him, a vindictive determination to see that she got what was coming to her. He'd see that no one in the town ever spoke to her again, the bitch! He'd see that everyone knew just what sort of floozy she was.

But by the time he had cleaver in hand and was dealing with a queue of women who had waited patiently for him to turn up, the mood had changed again. ('Touch of the flu,' he said, trying to be his normal cheery self, when customers commented on his appearance). He would think it all through, decide what to do about her. Because something had to be done. She couldn't go spreading that muck around this sleepy, conventional little town without someone putting the brakes on her.

It came to him as he prepared for bed that night that he needed advice, though from whom he could not imagine. His last waking memory was of that virago screaming at him from the bed where he thought he had found paradise. 'Sooky!' the haggard face shrieked. 'Softie! There aren't any men in this town…'

Kowalski fell asleep and dreamed tempestuous things.

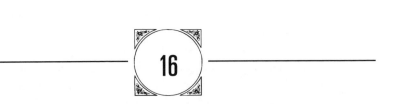

16

'So where do we stand, Sarge?' young Briggs asked. They were sitting across the desk in the office vacated by Pirt. 'Is it looking any clearer?'

Nick Verdun shuffled papers, producing one with tightly written detail covering both sides. 'Basically,' he said, 'the facts seem to be that the dagger had no fingerprints on it, the dressing room was out of people's vision for a very brief moment of time, and the deceased was probably one of the best-hated women in town.' He grinned humourlessly. 'It's not really enough.'

'What was she after? *Was* it blackmail?'

'No.' Verdun leaned back. 'It doesn't seem as if there was ever any money involved. Certainly the information turned in by the banks gave no indication of suspect payments in or out of accounts. It has to be power. She had them on strings, and when she wanted a bit of fun she pulled the string and—I assume—the puppet danced.'

'And then she pulled once too often and the puppet came at her with a knife?'

'That's how it looks to me.'

'Well, it shouldn't be too difficult to find him,' Briggs said with a certain lack of tact. 'That is...' He turned pink.

'I have been trying, you know,' Verdun said, mildly sarcastic. 'While you've been chatting up young ladies, *I* have been hard at work.'

'Only one,' said Briggs defensively. 'And I've done my own bit of hard yakka.'

'Did she know anything?'

'She warned me off.' Briggs grinned. 'Made a point of it.'

'Does that mean she doesn't know anything, or that she does?' Verdun mused. 'But why would she, anyway.'

'I bet there's not much goes on in these small towns that doesn't get out. Who are the best bets on your list?'

'My gut feeling says that it was a man,' Verdun said slowly. 'It has to be someone in that opera company, surely. She could have been knocked off so much more easily in her own study at the school. It almost seems as if it was a spur of the moment job, as if the opportunity presented itself and the deed was done. Simon Lee was checking that the front door was shut, and everyone else had left by the stage door. Except Miss Glencosset.' He stared ahead of him. 'Why was she so much longer than the others? Was she—was she expecting to meet someone? Hardly. She knew that Lee would want to lock up. He was always quite meticulous about it.'

'Maybe Lee was the one she wanted to see. She knew that they would be alone.'

Verdun stared at his offsider. 'Do you think so? It *was* his knife, after all. But surely he wouldn't...'

'He might.' Briggs was leaning forward eagerly. It was like a game, he was thinking, a game of chess, perhaps, with both sides trying to foretell the opponent's next move. Somewhere there was a person who had the answer right here in his brain (or hers, he reminded himself); what a pity no one had discovered how to X-ray the mind and reveal its secrets. 'Who's in the running, boss?'

'There's quite a handful who turn up over and over again in the diaries. If they are all local people, and I think they must be, then they are all in the hot seat. But she kept it deliberately obscure. I can't relate the initials she used to anyone here.' He ran his eyes down the notes. 'Besides, as far as she made any definite accusations they hardly seem to be the stuff of which murder is made. More malicious spite than anything, I should have said.'

'Nothing to report to HQ, then?'

Verdun grimaced. 'Don't! It's a sore point. The general impression at HQ seems to be that if it happens in a country town there's no problem. Happy peasants dancing in a ring, that's what they think it's like. But this lot's as devious as any city bunch.'

'"uman naycher!' Briggs said facetiously. 'Country bumpkins are off.' He hesitated. 'It's all right, I suppose, if I happen to meet Natalie Percy sort of accidentally, sir? Protocol won't be outraged?'

'*I* might be.' Verdun sat back and regarded the young man. 'A murder investigation is a very sensitive affair.'

'I know.' He looked glum for a moment and then brightened up. 'But she might know something—something that no one else knows. It could be my duty to extract that information from her.'

Verdun sighed. 'I knew it was a mistake to bring an adolescent Romeo with me. You can see her in the line of duty, Briggs, but anything else *must* wait until afterwards—and particularly until we know she's not involved.'

Briggs frowned. 'She couldn't be! I'd stake my reputation on it.'

Verdun laughed out loud, swinging himself out of Pirt's uncomfortable chair. 'What reputation, Constable Briggs? I didn't bring you here to check out the talent.' He became solemn. 'You're here to discover who pushed a dagger into a middle-aged lady's back—and why? When you've solved it, then you can start having a "reputation"!' He patted the boy's shoulder. 'Come on—we're going to pay a visit to Chester Parkinson, the chemist. Bring your notebook—you can impress him with your efficiency.'

Michael Kowalski stood inside the bare hall of the rectory, where little more than Mrs Bedwell's 'lick and a promise' had been seen in years. There was a sharp temperature drop as the front door closed behind him; it seemed as if, with the closing, the air grew thin, irradiated by faint aromas of damp and decay, of burnt meat pies and the cheapest brands of instant coffee.

He stood, battered Akubra in hand, staring down the narrow hallway, its once cream-painted walls punctuated by mission-brown doors. There was no sound but a strange, irregular clicking, and Kowalski followed it to a room at the far end of the corridor, where it revealed itself as the Rev Charles on his typewriter, which he operated on a kind of search-and-attack principle. Hanging over the small manual machine, one finger poised ready to descend, his shoulders bunched in his ancient black alpaca jacket, he had the look of a vulture waiting for its next meal to die. As Kowalski watched, the finger descended, and the vicar, peering disconsolately at the paper, said 'Damn!'

His sudden irritated movement brought the butcher into his line of vision. For a moment he stared as at an apparition; then a strange expression crossed his sallow face. As he rose, slowly and stiffly, he was in turn confused and angry, alarmed and defensive, and a faint blush indicated that the blood was flowing with a greater than usual passion.

Kowalski gestured heavily towards the typewriter. 'Sorry if I've interrupted you, Vicar. I knocked...' he continued his gesture towards the front door, 'and I rang. But you didn't hear.'

'The bell isn't working.' The Rev Charles seemed to have some of the Rectory dust in his throat. He swallowed. 'Hasn't worked for years.' He stared balefully at the young man. Of all the people (and there were many) he would have preferred *not* to see at this moment, Kowalski could well have headed the list.

'Good old machines, the Remingtons,' the butcher said, trying to generate some warmth into the occasion. The vicar stared, following Kowalski's eyes, and nodded vaguely. But all he could see was Molly, Molly's lively, impish face, Molly's ripely curving body, Molly's bright clothes and brighter eyes. He swallowed a groan. Those eyes! Always laughing at him, encouraging him, then closing with a snap like Mrs Bedwell's handbag, shutting him out, leaving him bereft—turning him on! He faced Kowalski.

'What can I do for you?' He waved towards a chair, and the visitor sat down awkwardly, thighs too broad for the narrow arms, feet squarely planted on the cheap rug, Akubra turning, turning, in fists like legs of lamb.

'I gotta talk to someone,' Kowalski began, eyes down in embarrassment. 'I been trying to think it out on me own, but it won't go. So I thought of you! Well, it's your sort o' job, isn't it—listening to people? People in trouble. So I thought, well, I'll go and see the reverend, and he'll know what to do.' He regarded the vicar furtively, beginning to doubt the wisdom of his visit.

'Of course,' said the Rev Charles, pulling himself together. 'Any way I can help—any way at all—of course—glad to.' He waited, trying to pretend that this overweight young person of somewhat cloddish disposition was not the paramour of his darling.

'Well, it's like this—and don't think I like doing this, reverend, because I don't...' Memory showed Kowalski Molly de Vance, siren, enticing him into her bed on that first night of nights, her body sleek in peach satin, and he gulped. 'It's like this...'

'Yes?' the vicar was apprehensive. What on earth was he about to hear?

'Well, to cut a long story short...you know Molly de Vance?'

The vicar gave a short of half-hatched hiccup. 'Molly...'

'*You* know—in the chorus. Mikado chorus. You know?'

'Yes,' said the Rev Charles. 'I know.'

'Some information has come into my hands. Regarding Molly.' He looked up, stolidly virtuous. He'd put paid to the silly bitch! 'I thought I ought to bring it to you.'

The Rev Charles Culbert felt his knees grow weak. 'He knows!' he was thinking desperately. 'He knows! And now he's going to blackmail me. And I shall be disgraced. And have to leave. And find another job. And be despised and rejected of men...!' He took a deep breath, forcing his panic-filled mind to slow down, hold on to reason. He heard his voice, only a little strained, say, 'Quite right, my boy!'

'Molly sometimes goes on holiday, somewhere in south-east Asia. Penang once, Bali, a couple of times to Singapore.' Culbert nodded, confused. 'Well—she brings stuff back with her!' Kowalski sat back, brimming with satisfaction. He'd got it out!

'Stuff?' the vicar was even more perplexed.

'You know—what people bring back.' He smirked. It felt better, sharing the knowledge.

'Duty-free, you mean?'

Kowalski laughed shortly. 'Oh, yes, it's duty-free! It's duty-free all right.'

Culbert felt he was drowning in innuendo. 'Cameras, you mean? Whisky?'

Michael Kowalski leaned forward urgently.

'Come on, Vicar! You know what I mean.' He stared into the pale, anxious eyes. 'Drugs, Reverend! Illegal drugs.'

The Rev Charles knew his mouth was opening and closing foolishly, but it seemed he had no control over it. Kowalski was sitting back, nodding fatuously. Culbert thought he might draw his fist back and let it fly into the butcher's fat face, that he might take up the poker from the hearth and smash it down on the thick skull, or even rush into the kitchen and find the carving knife and... He closed his eyes in agony. What was he doing? What was he thinking? 'I don't believe it,' he heard himself say.

'It's true enough,' Kowalski said smugly. 'I've—seen it.' No point in telling the old boy that he'd shared some of it during that second shattering night. (And would never use it again, that's for sure). 'She and I was—well, like *that* for a while.'

'Was? Oh, dear! Oh-dear-oh-dear!' Culbert stood, moving agitatedly around the cramped little study. He turned to look at Kowalski. 'What is it you want from me? What do you expect me to do?'

'Well, it's like doctors, isn't it? Like the confessional in the other lot.' He was referring to St Francis of Assisi's R.C. church at the far end of town. 'I mean, I can tell you and it doesn't have to go any further. Know what I mean?' He gave a heart-felt sigh. 'I feel better already. Getting it off my chest.' He stood, holding out his huge hand, and Culbert, mesmerised, shook it limply.

'My pleasure, young man. My pleasure...'

'A trouble shared is a trouble halved—that's what they say, eh? Well, good on yer, Vicar. I'll see myself out.'

The Rev Charles listened as the footsteps receded, the door opened and closed. He wondered if he would ever be able to move again. A strange immobility seemed to have seized his legs. But suddenly they gave way beneath him, and he collapsed on to a chair, shaking uncontrollably.

'Molly!' he groaned. 'Molly...! *Set me as a seal upon thy heart, as a seal upon thy arm: for love is strong as death; jealousy—is cruel as the grave...*' After a long silence pulsating with his anguish he stirred and went back to the desk. He stared down blankly at the paper, not comprehending what he saw. Molly's face danced before him, and he tried to banish her with a wide, ungainly movement of hand and arm; but she was not to be dealt with lightly. She led his eyes back to the text he had chosen for the coming Sunday: *Though your sins be as scarlet, they shall be white as snow.* Violently he tore the paper out of the machine and threw it with futile rage into the empty fireplace. '*Thou art weighed in the balances,*' he muttered through clenched teeth, '*and art found wanting*'! (And there came from somewhere in the back of the Rectory the sound like the rush of a torrent in spate: it was the Reverend Charles Culbert, BD, man of God, weeping and wailing and gnashing his teeth in solitary fury).

17

Nick Verdun and young Briggs entered the pharmacy, trying to look like customers. Bella, dabbing at the cosmetics counter with a feather duster, saw them come through the door and felt a tremor of alarm. But she came forward sweetly enough, her chemist's-wife smile carefully affixed, and asked them what she could do for them.

'I'd like a word with Mr Parkinson,' Verdun said, glancing around him and locating Chester behind the glass screen of the dispensing department.

'Mr Parkinson will not keep you long,' she said graciously. 'He is just dispensing a prescription. Would you care to come through to the back?'

They followed her through the door marked 'private' and she invited them to sit down. 'I'll tell Chester you're here.' She closed the door as she left.

'He knows we're here,' Briggs said, *sotto voce*. 'He was watching us all the way.' They sat in silence, Verdun getting his thoughts in order, Briggs pondering the fact that in another moment or two a murderer might come through that door; he was still new enough to detecting not to have become used to meeting a known murderer face to face.

Chester Parkinson entered slowly and shut the door behind him, glancing from Verdun to Briggs and back again without speaking. 'Yes?' he said at last. 'How can I help you?'

'In the matter of Miss Glencosset's death,' Verdun began with a slight trace of pomposity that made young Briggs turn his head, 'I have a small piece of evidence, which I think you may be able to help me with. It is in regard to some phone calls made by Miss Glencosset on the afternoon of the day she was killed.' It interested him to see that Parkinson could not quite meet his eye. 'She had made a list of phone numbers, and yours was one of them.'

Chester Parkinson swallowed drily, feeling his heart give a great lurch in his breast. Here it was, then! Discovery, shame, penury! 'Yes?' he said without expression.

'Do you recall having such a call from the deceased?'

The chemist let his eyes wander around the room, hoping that he looked like an honest man trying to remember a past detail, but suspecting that he simply looked devious. 'Not at the moment.'

'It would help us if we could find out what she was phoning about,' Verdun said encouragingly. 'Any information, however small, may prove to be useful.' He glanced towards the closed door. 'Perhaps Mrs Parkinson...?'

'No!' Chester almost shot forward in his agitation. 'No! You are not to speak to my wife. I forbid it! Absolutely!'

Verdun raised his eyebrows. The reaction was out of keeping. 'If your wife has information she is required to give it to us.'

'I remember now,' Parkinson said, his voice shaken. 'She—Miss Glencosset did ring me on the afternoon of—of her death. She— she wanted me to make up a prescription for her.'

'Ah,' said Verdun, smiling. 'That would account for it. And did you?'

'Did I?'

'Did you make up the prescription?'

'I—well, of course I did.'

'Good.' Verdun was positively congratulatory. 'Good! And when did you give it to her?'

'I—er—oh...' Chester Parkinson's gaze flew around the room like a trapped bird. 'I don't recall.'

'Did she call for it? Here, at the shop?'

'No—no, I think not.'

'Then when...? What arrangement did you make?'

'I said—I said I would give it to her at the dress rehearsal later on.'

'And did you?' Verdun was alarmingly bland.

For a moment the chemist looked angry. 'Really, I have more on my mind than remembering exactly what I did on one afternoon last week, Sergeant!' He strode defiantly across the room and stood with his back to the window—('*So that I can't see his face properly*,' Verdun thought, grinning to himself).

'Rather a special day, I should have thought,' he said calmly. 'Everyone getting ready for the big moment at the theatre, and then, later on, the murder of one of the cast. Enough to make it stand out in your mind?'

'Enough to make one forget trivial details!' Parkinson shot back.

Verdun stood slowly. 'Well, thank you, Mr Parkinson,' he said courteously, preparing to leave. 'At least you were able to confirm that Miss Glencosset had rung you. It makes it likely that she rang the others on the list, too.' At the door he stopped and turned back. 'By the way, what *was* the prescription?'

Parkinson stared at him. 'What?'

'The bottle you were making up for Miss Glencosset. What was it? If I know what we're looking for it'll make it a lot easier.'

He felt quite sorry for the man. The grey cheeks suddenly flared pink, and the eyes, which had grown aggressive, lost their brave sparkle. 'It was a...a...'he began. 'It was...'

'Yes?' Verdun waited patiently.

'It was a—a cough mixture. One of my own recipes. A herbal thing.'

'She had a cough, did she? A nuisance for her, if she had to sing.'

'A—a preventative,' said the hapless chemist.

'Ah,' said Verdun, leaving the meaning open. 'Good idea. Nothing like being prepared. Does it have a name?'

'I call it "No-coff",' Parkinson muttered. He led the way into the shop, desperate to get rid of them.

'One of these?' young Briggs asked, picking up a dark bottle from a basket placed in a strategic position.

'Yes, that's the one.' He looked so miserable Verdun wished he didn't have to go on. Across the shop Bella Parkinson was still dusting, but her eyes were fixed on her husband.

'And you took one of these to the theatre that night and gave it to Miss Glencosset?'

'Yes.'

Verdun, no slouch himself when it came to acting, turned and pierced Briggs with a steely eye. 'You missed that, Briggs,' he accused. 'Go back to the theatre and find that bottle.' Briggs, much astonished, gave a kind of salute and slipped away hurriedly. 'Well,' Verdun said, turning back to Chester, whose face had gone from grey to chalk, 'thank you for your assistance. I'll see myself out.'

Briggs was waiting round the corner. 'I haven't got a key,' he said, puzzled. 'Do you really want me to go over that place again?'

Verdun hustled him away. 'No. That's all window dressing. I don't believe for a moment that it was a bottle of medicine that she rang him about. But I'm damned sure there was something secretive and shady going on. Come on, let's visit the next one.'

Briggs, hurrying to keep up, said, 'What list did you find?'

'It was tucked in her current diary, folded like a book mark. I almost didn't look at it. But it was done that afternoon. There was a reference to it on the page. Something like *"cat now among pigeons. Calls made. Now we'll see who has the upper hand!"* Tragic, really. A sort of preparation for her own death.'

Briggs was overtaken by an unexpectedly vivid sense of the drama in which he found himself a bit player. 'Makes you stop and think, doesn't it? She thought she'd got it all weighed up.'

'Let it be a lesson to you,' Verdun said. 'Keep to the straight and narrow!'

Driving away in the car, Briggs asked, 'Who else was on the phone list?'

'Good question. Quite a few, I'm afraid. And I really am afraid that one of them, as they say, did her in!'

'But you don't know yet which one?'

Verdun nodded slowly. 'I don't know. But I'm beginning to make educated guesses.'

'Let's see.' Briggs frowned in concentration. 'People she had something on. People she presumably knew quite well. Probably people involved with G and S. You think it was a man?' He paused. 'How far back do these entries go?'

'Years! She'd been the arch sticky-beak of all time, as far as I can tell. A nasty, interfering woman—that's how it looks. And for some reason, on that afternoon, she decided to give the pot a stir.' Verdun watched the passing scenery with half an eye. 'Why? What was she trying to do? What did she hope to gain?'

18

When Natalie left the supermarket that afternoon, Briggs was waiting. 'You again?' she said, wary, though not entirely displeased, for young Briggs was a good-looking youth. 'Doesn't that boss of yours give you enough to do?' The shyness was evaporating.

'He sent me,' Briggs said, looking smug. 'He wants me to ask you something. Where can we go?'

'You can ask it right here,' she said, coming to a halt among the home-going shoppers. 'No funny business!'

'Not here,' he said firmly. 'Come and sit in the park.' This was an area of neatly trimmed grass in the middle of town. Her curiosity getting the better of her, Natalie allowed herself to be guided to a bench. They sat down, and Briggs pulled out his notepad; Natalie's eyebrows rose slightly.

'This is dinkum, then? You really want to talk to me about—you know?'

'Right!' He opened the pad and looked down at the question he had scribbled below at Nick Verdun's dictation. 'Sergeant Verdun wants to know—after you said goodnight to Miss Glencosset, exactly what did you do?' He looked up.

'I went home.'

'No—more exactly than that. You went out of the dressing room, leaving her there, then…?'

'Then I went through the Green Room to the back door. *Then* I went home.'

'After the back door, what then?'

'Look, what is this?' she said, petulantly. 'I told him all this before.'

'Not in detail. Sorry! It's got to be done. Because you were the last to see her…'

'Here!' She stared at him anxiously. 'You don't think *I* did it, do you?'

He longed to say that of course she couldn't have done it, that it was quite out of the question. But Verdun had warned him. Professional approach, give nothing away. 'It's not possible to rule anyone out at this juncture,' he replied pompously, and she looked at him thoughtfully and then give a quick nod of the head.

'Then I'd better be careful what I say.' She stared at the ground, thinking. 'I went through the stage door.'

'Did you see anyone then?'

'I could hear Simon Lee going up to the back of the auditorium to check the doors. He's a real fusspot! No one uses those doors at rehearsal, but he checks them all the same.'

'Always?'

'Every time! Why?'

'Any diversion from normal behaviour could be a clue.'

'Well, that was quite normal for him, I can tell you. Proper old woman, he is. Then—well, when I got outside there were a few people about, but it's hard to see who's there, because the lighting's bad in the car-park. I did see Jasper. He was waiting for Maggie. She usually gets fish and chips for them after a rehearsal. And there were cars going off in all directions. I passed a couple of people while I was going round into the main street.'

'Who were they?'

She shrugged. 'I don't think I noticed. The Harcourts had gone, I think, and I saw the Parkinsons leave together, of course.'

She looked at him slyly. 'Siamese twins, the Parkinsons. Though how anyone would want to be tied to...'

'All right,' Briggs said. 'No personalities. Who else?'

'Corinne was with Maggie, I think. I saw them as I passed the chippery. Pattie? I think she'd gone already. Not with Dave Shafto, though. Least, I don't think so. I heard his bike taking off up the road when I got round to the front of the theatre.'

'He left after you?'

'I don't think so. Unless he was hiding...' She stopped, putting her hand to her mouth. 'Oh, I didn't mean that. Honest! I've no idea where he was, but I don't think he was in the theatre.'

Briggs wrote in his notebook, flipping the pages over as he scribbled. 'Did anybody go back into the building while you were there?'

She shook her head slowly. 'I don't think so.' Suddenly she straightened up, glaring at him as if he himself was the guilty party. 'I hate this!' she exclaimed. 'I hate all the questions. What are you trying to do—make me dob in a friend?'

He regarded her with sympathy and a flicker of embarrassment. 'I hate it too. Let's walk.' He stood and held out a hand to her. But she ignored it, walking past him with determination.

'Not with you, thanks. Not while this thing's going on. Everybody'll think I'm not to be trusted. I'll lose all my friends because of you. It's not worth it.' And she was gone, striding irritably across the green grass, losing herself in the crowd. Briggs watched her go and heaved a sigh. A policeman's lot was not a happy one.

Across the road a pair of eyes narrowed as Briggs put his notebook away and strolled back to the car.

It was Bingo Rafferty's proud boast that nothing got wasted while he was around to find a use for it. Need a pirate boat? Bingo had just the materials to construct the prow of a splendidly swelling galleon, which, with the ropes he had 'appropriated' from one place and some ancient yacht sails he had 'liberated' from another, would make any audience believe in what they were seeing.

Need a dungeon? A rocky promontory? A fairy glen? Bingo would have what was needed, somewhere in the vast representation of chaos he called 'home'. Of course, his skills were not only required by the annual activities of the G and S society; his true vocation lay in 'dealing', and it mattered not what he dealt in, somehow he would always find just enough to live on, to eat and especially to drink. He was that rare creature, a contented man.

He had, on this particularly lovely day, an order (strictly against the law, but so mildly illegal that it never occurred to him to refuse) for some of the wild flower plants that grew in profusion on the far side of the creek from town. This was the walk that Nanki-Poo had taken with his Yum-Yum only a few days before, and it led Bingo along a sandy track to a wooden bridge, which crossed the creek at its widest part.

Kangaroo paws abounded, and he lifted a dozen or so of the plants before reaching the bridge, dropping them into a large hessian bag he hung across his shoulders. At the bridge he stopped for a moment, for Bingo was by no means without a sensitive soul, and the view from there was particularly pleasant. So exceedingly pleasant was it, in fact, that he leaned against the rickety parapet of the bridge and took time to savour it, and the scented aroma of the bush. Which was when he realised that something was lying in the shallow water, something big enough to be a human body, and not the bundle of refuse he had first thought it.

Bingo Rafferty had shown no fear in Korea; he had faced a stampede of buffalo in the Northern Territory and lain all night in the bush in exquisite pain after a snake bite without losing his cool. But now he broke out in a sweat as he contemplated climbing down into the creek and hauling the body to the bank. *Old age*, he muttered to himself; *that's what it is*. You can't do when you're seventy what you can do when you're forty. He had no doubt that this was, indeed, a corpse; face down in the peaty brown water of the creek, it was bedraggled and water-logged. He looked around for help, but without much hope. The whole reason he had taken this path was that, except at weekends, he could be virtually certain of meeting no one.

Then he thought of the policeman, the one who was investigating the murder. Now he'd have another to pry into. Bingo had never counted the police as among his closest friends, but at this traumatic time he felt they might like to justify their existence. He took a last look at the body, wedged against the bank where the undergrowth hung over, and made it with reasonable haste back to where he had parked his ute.

True to type, they seemed to suspect him, when all he was trying to do was bring a malfeasance to their notice. They—the detective Verdun and that clodhopper Pirt—warned him to say nothing, to stay within the town limits until they had had a chance to talk with him, and to discuss this with no one.

Perhaps the final injunction was the hardest to bear. Bingo was by nature garrulous, and when the drink was in him, warm and benevolently tongue-loosening, he was in his element. He went back to his cluttered empire and sat on his ramshackle veranda, waiting his call to the police presence (and suddenly remembering that he had left his plants lying there by the creek)—meanwhile drinking what was left of a carton of beer that had fallen off the tail of someone's utility a few weeks back along the main road.

Before he got to the singing stage, he suddenly realised that he still didn't know who it was lying there in the creek, alone and friendless.

But Nick Verdun knew. And, after an agonised glance, young Briggs knew too, leaning over the flower-decked bank to heave with shock and revulsion. Natalie Percy had been dead for several hours, and there were dark, ugly marks on her neck where she had had the life pressed out of her. Above the temple, across which straggled hair lay like strands of water weed, was a purple wound that showed up with ghastly emphasis against the dead white face.

'Why?' Briggs said, clasping his head in his hands. 'Why would anyone?'

'God knows!' Nick, though toughened by experience, was deeply saddened as he stood above the body, staring down at it, wondering what the last thoughts in that broken head had been, what terror had borne her off into eternity.

He could echo Briggs's 'why' with his own. What had Natalie known that had made it necessary to destroy her? For he had no doubt that his instinct was correct when it told him that the two murders must be connected

The doctor's report made it clear that the blow to the head had probably stunned her, and that she had been strangled while she was unconscious. 'Thank God,' whispered Briggs, pale with shock and anger. Verdun had offered to send him back to HQ, to bring someone down to replace him; but after the initial despair had worn off a grimly mature expression had come to replace the youthful exuberance. 'I'll stay,' he had said to Verdun. 'I'll find the bugger that did this...!'

'We are not into retribution,' the sergeant warned him. 'We are detectives, not executioners. If you have the slightest belief that you won't be able to handle this like any other case, you must say so. I can't afford to have an avenging angel on the job.'

Briggs's teeth were clenched. 'I'll behave properly, sir,' he said through them. 'My thoughts are my own. But you've got to let me stay. I shan't be able to live with myself otherwise.'

Verdun regarded him curiously. 'Were you that keen on her?'

'It's not that. She was a nice girl. I had a bit of fun flirting with her, nothing more. But she was probably killed because someone saw her with me. Don't you think so, Sarge? Someone thought she was telling me something dangerous to them.'

'Who?'

'I don't know. But I intend to find out.'

'OK.' Verdun leaned back wearily. 'Tell me again what she told you. Do you think she knew who had killed Glencosset?'

'No. I'm sure she didn't. But maybe my questions reminded her of something she'd forgotten. It's not impossible.'

'Would she have come to you with it?'

'I don't know.' Briggs stared at Verdun. He went again through what Natalie had told him, referring to his notes; and when he had finished they looked thoughtfully at each other.

'It's not all that helpful,' Verdun said finally. 'But it means that young Shafto isn't quite in the clear—he might just have had time to slip inside, kill Miss G. and scoot off before Lee got back to the Green Room. Whoever did it was mighty slick.'

'Can we go over it again? Who was there at the end of the dress rehearsal? Apart from Natalie and the deceased and Simon Lee?'

Verdun brought out the paper with a list of names on it. 'The ones who were actually left when the rest were gone were…'

Briggs interrupted him. 'But surely someone could have come back? Someone could have waited outside in the shadows and then slipped inside. Someone who had left, perhaps, straight after the rehearsal was finished. One of the back-stage people.'

'Bingo Rafferty,' Verdun said. 'Chester Parkinson. Not back-stage exactly, but with an interest. Simon Lee. Mary Harcourt, Dulcet Merridew. Jasper and Maggie Spenlow. And a handful of scene-shifters and others, any of whom, I suppose, could be in the running.'

'You really believe it's all connected with those diaries, don't you?' This was a new Briggs, intense, pale-faced, not to be diverted. Verdun nodded sombrely.

'I do. As far as motive goes, it's the only link we have. That, and the fact that she was a member of the G and S. If only we could locate the people she mentions!'

'It couldn't just have been an accident that it all got mixed up with Mikado?'

'If it is,' Verdun declared with some energy, 'I'll go back on the beat!'

Briggs managed a pale smile. 'Nothing's that bad, Sarge.'

'You see,' Verdun said abstractedly, his mind chasing stray thoughts through a morass of confusion, 'I'm sure she rang them up on that afternoon. I'm certain she precipitated her own death. It's a gut feeling. I can't explain it. *But*—if she was killed by someone from outside the society, would it have happened then? There would be any number of opportunities for a woman living virtually on her own to be murdered. It may the killer's big mistake—to limit the suspects to one group of people.' He closed his eyes, thinking deeply. 'One of them did it. But which?'

19

Sylvia Milton regarded the detectives with suspicion. She was sure they were up to no good where Mr Harcourt was concerned.

Her recent tearful collapse was still burning in her memory, but she had herself well under control now and would behave impeccably, as long as others would do the same. 'Yes?' she said now to the two men, raising her eyebrows forbiddingly.

'We would like to see Mr Harcourt,' Verdun said with winning charm. Sylvia sniffed in decorous fashion, just enough to let him know that she was not impressed.

'Mr Harcourt is busy. He can see no one.'

'He will see me,' Verdun said authoritatively. 'Police business.'

Sylvia rose slowly from her chair, determined not to be hurried. 'I will see,' she said coolly, approaching the hallowed door.

'Did you know,' Verdun said with a touch of brutality, 'that Natalie Percy is dead?' Her reaction was instant; her eyes shot open and the cool demeanour left her. With one hand on Harcourt's door she stopped, staring at Verdun and then at Briggs with horror.

'No!' she said, her voice no more than a whisper. 'No! Oh, that's terrible. What was it—a car?'

'Murder,' Verdun said without expression.

Sylvia moved slowly to her chair and sat down again. There was a look of total incomprehension on her ashen face. '*Murder? Natalie? But who—why? Was she...?*' She flinched from the word.

'No, she wasn't raped. It wasn't that kind of murder. We believe it may have connections with Miss Glencosset's death. And if we are to solve it we shall need the cooperation of everyone in this town.' He smiled grimly. 'Please tell Mr Harcourt I wish to see him.'

'Yes, of course...' She went swiftly to Harcourt's door and opened it, closing it behind her. Through the glass Verdun could see her bending over the desk, speaking to Harcourt; his head came up suddenly, his eyes going to where the two detectives were standing. He stood and came to the door.

'What's this? What's happened? Natalie Percy...surely not.'

'Unfortunately...' Verdun began, making his purposeful way into the office and leaving Briggs behind. The door closed, shutting out further sound. Briggs turned to Sylvia.

'We need to know the movements of anyone who might have had a connection with these two deaths,' he began. Sylvia, recovering slightly, bristled.

'You surely don't think I...'

'Probably not.' This new, harder, seasoned Briggs seemed to have lost his cheery smile. 'But I'll have the details anyway. And then Mr Harcourt's.'

'Ask him,' she said with a spurt of anger.

Briggs stared her out. 'I'm asking you,' he said clearly. 'What time did you leave here yesterday?'

By the time Verdun and Briggs met to compare notes they had a fair outline of people's movements since closing time the previous afternoon. A shocked population seemed at last to be taking the case seriously. Miss Glencosset's death had been an excitement, a dramatic interlude involving someone for whom most had had little time. But Natalie was young and nice-looking, and she was known throughout the town as the pretty girl at the check-out in the supermarket.

Natalie, they would remember, always had a shy word for everyone. Natalie liked the boys but knew how to behave with decorum. Natalie never forgot to ask after people's aching bones and far-flung grandchildren. She would be sadly missed. That someone could have killed her so barbarically was beyond comprehension. This was tragedy, where the previous murder had been something of a nine days' wonder, a break from dull routine.

Verdun sat far into the night, wrestling with the diaries and their enigmatic secrets. Briggs, not wishing to sleep, drew up timetables from the information he had gleaned during the day, matching them against each other, looking for weaknesses, for coincidences: looking for a murderer!

Maggie glanced across the breakfast table at her husband. 'Why did the sergeant want to see you again?' she asked curiously.

He shrugged. 'Obviously they believe the two deaths are connected. They're taking their time coming up with a solution.' He turned the newspaper to another page. 'They reckon they're interviewing everyone again.'

Maggie stirred her coffee slowly. 'Who do you think did it?'

'How would I know? I'm not in their confidence.'

'Poor Natalie!' Maggie sighed. 'What a dreadful thing.'

'These girls will go wandering around at dead of night,' Jasper said unsympathetically. 'It's not surprising if they get themselves knocked off.'

'That's a terrible thing to say, Jasper!' She glared at him. 'Girls should be able to walk about whenever they want. There is absolutely no reason why a woman should have to skulk indoors because there may be a rampaging man on the prowl. What sort of society do we live in, anyway?'

'A rotten society,' Jasper said, folding the newspaper and putting it on the floor. 'Where no one is safe. Didn't you know? Haven't you read about it? More coffee!'

'You make me sick,' Maggie said, though quite calmly, as if the idea were nothing new. She poured another cup. 'Presumably they think the same person is responsible for both killings.' She shuddered. 'How dreadful to think that someone we know...'

'Well, we don't really know any of them that well,' Jasper said. 'Not outside the G and S. Though that doesn't make them murderers, of course.'

'*I* know some of them very well. I get on with them. Not close, maybe, but...'

'Getting close to you,' he said, deliberately spiteful, 'is a virtual impossibility.'

'Charming!' Maggie smiled at him mockingly. 'So early in the morning, too.' She put her head on one side, examining his face. 'At least I know you couldn't have done it.'

He stared at her. 'What the hell do you mean?'

'You wouldn't need to stab and bash and drown. You could just spit on them. Pure vitriol! Pure poison, darling. Probably the perfect crime. How would they charge you? "That on Wednesday last you did cause the death of one Pretty Polly Perkins by spitting on her"!' She laughed, getting to her feet to clear the table. 'Anyway,' she murmured, her voice provocatively low and sweet, 'you wouldn't have the guts. That's a comfort! You should tell Sergeant Verdun. "I don't have the guts, Sergeant!" Then he could cross you straight off his little list.'

Jasper watched her go into the kitchen, his face pale with the effort of not answering back. Why, he asked himself passionately, had no one come along and beaten the living daylights out of that harridan? Where was justice?

20

Simon Lee was deeply worried, as was quite natural under the circumstances. He felt in some way responsible for this latest monstrous act of murder, though why he was not really sure. It was something to do with Natalie Percy being young, and in the G and S, and he himself being president—and he knew that that gave him no right over other members' lives, but he did wish he had taken the trouble to warn the younger women, especially, that until the killer was caught they should take particular care.

He had arrived home from a couple of days with his sister on the coast; within minutes his front door bell had been rung by the sergeant, wishing to know where he had been etcetera...It was a matter of thankfulness that there were plenty of people able to vouch for him, for on that night when Natalie Percy was being robbed of life he had been playing cards with his sister's neighbours at a distance from the scene of nearly three hundred kilometres.

'Is there any way I can help, Sergeant Verdun?' he asked in his normal slightly anxious manner. 'This is a terrible thing. It must be cleared up.'

'There are several people who are not able to confirm their movements on the night before last.' He regarded Lee thoughtfully. 'If I am right, sir, this death hinges on the first. And if so, then you are in the clear. I can eliminate you from the list, then I shall be glad to have your assistance. Local knowledge is very important.'

Simon hesitated. 'It wasn't Bingo, was it?'

'I doubt it. Why?'

'I don't know. I wouldn't have liked it to be Bingo.' He gave a small, sad smile. 'But then, I really don't know anyone I would actually like it to be. Oh, dear!'

Briggs had spent his day doggedly going over the ground again and again. There was a heat in him, a passionate anger that Natalie's death should ever have happened. He was determined to find out why. He knew now where everyone *said* they were at the time the doctor believed the girl had been killed; he knew the sideways glances, the nervousness that could have been either guilt or simply embarrassment; he knew the feeling, too, of the hunting dog that gets the scent, that puts its nose down and cannot be stopped, once the trail has been laid.

Verdun had gone over Natalie's rooms, not wanting Briggs to have that disturbing experience under the circumstances; searching through a young woman's belongings was not one of his favourite pastimes, but it had to be done. Her property was much as he could have guessed: chain store clothes, attractive but mass-produced; cosmetics from a medium price range; a couple of soft toys left over from childhood; some letters and post-cards from friends who had gone to Bali and New Zealand and Hong Kong. Not a hoarder, young Natalie—only one bundle of papers: a passport, birth certificate and so on. They were in a large envelope, unaddressed, and Verdun took them away to go through them slowly.

He awoke suddenly in the middle of the night: they had missed something. Where was her handbag? Surely she had been carrying one? It was the one thing a woman could be guaranteed to own, and to carry at all times. So where was Natalie's?

Bingo, now a celebrity in his own right, sat at the bar of his favourite watering hole and told the tale for the umpteenth time. 'There she was, floating down the stream like that lass in "Hamlet", forget her name, surrounded by water weeds and her little hands lying pale in the water like fish.' He was growing more poetic by the minute. His audience begged him to go on.

Briggs, sitting unnoticed in a corner with his one drink of the evening, put up with the inane chatter as long as he could bear it, then sallied forth to the bar. 'Bingo Rafferty,' he said, his voice coldly official, 'if you have information you haven't given to the police I shall have to take you in for questioning.'

Bingo looked up through a pleasantly pink haze and was unabashed. 'Ah,' he said, emitting enough spirituous fumes to start a car, 'it's the young'un! My shout, young'un!' He raised a hand to call the barman, but Briggs was too quick for him.

'When did you see the—the body...' (he hardly even stammered over the word), '*floating* down the creek?'

'Well...' Bingo began with the bluster of the habitually found out. 'Perhaps floating was a bit of exaggeration. More like caught in the reeds. But I found her, didn't I?' He grinned triumphantly. 'It was me what found her.'

Briggs stared at him coolly. 'You certainly did. That may not incriminate you, but I should watch it if I were you, Rafferty. The sergeant's hot on the trail.' He let his eyes wander round Bingo's small audience. 'Hot!' he said with finality, and left.

'Here,' said one of Bingo's mates, '*you* didn't do it, did you?' Rafferty, his good name impugned, waved a fist. But Briggs had undermined his little piece of drama, and his mates wandered off and looked for something new to drink to. Bingo called for another beer and felt sorely used.

'I found her,' he mumbled to the barman. 'It was me what found her.'

The barman pushed his glass across the jarrah surface. 'That might not have been very clever of you, mate. Police get very suspicious of blokes that find bodies.'

Bingo, his evening ruined, drank up quickly and went off. Perhaps Dulcet Merridew was at home.

She was; but she wasn't pleased to see Bingo, certainly not in his sozzled state.

'Do go home, Bingo,' she said through the crack of the door. He could see the chain on. 'You're in no state to go visiting. Go home, there's a dear.'

'But, Dulce...' he began. Dulcet, however, was adamant

'*Go home*, Bingo dear. At once. The police won't be at all pleased if they know you're wandering around knocking on young ladies' doors.'

'I'm not,' he moaned. 'I'm knocking on yours.'

Even for Dulcet, this was a bit much. 'If you don't go home, Bingo, I shall ring Sergeant Verdun. Don't you understand, you silly man?' She was suddenly angry. 'Natalie's been killed!'

'I found her,' Bingo began, glad to have another opportunity.

'I know you found her. But until her killer has been found, too, no one in their right mind is going to open the door at night to a *man*! And certainly not to someone as drunk as you are, Bingo, dear. Now, go home, there's a good fellow.'

Bingo stared at the door. 'You mean...?'

'I mean that until the sergeant has the murderer locked up we *have to take care!*'

'But—*you* don't think it was me, do you, Dulce?' He felt suddenly quite alarmed. If Dulce could suspect him, how could he prove to her—to the police... 'Do you, Dulce?'

'Of course not, Bingo,' she said through the gap, relenting a little. 'But I can't be sure, can I? So go...'

He turned away, somewhat sobered. The understanding that he was behaving like an idiot came slowly, but it arrived at last. He walked unsteadily down to the gate, turning there to see that Dulcet had closed the door and was standing outlined against the window. Gloomily he waved a hand to her before trudging off down the road. It was some time before he realised that he had no idea where he had left his vehicle.

Pirt, jolted out of his daily rural routine, gathered his small force of police and sent them off, all around the town, to search for Natalie's handbag. The creek, soon muddied by wading feet in very large rubber boots, revealed nothing. Accessible bush gave up no secrets. Privacy was invaded, from Rafferty's abominable area of visual pollution to the neat homes of Mary Harcourt and Bella Parkinson.

'What was it like, again?' Verdun said, and Briggs closed his eyes to aid memory.

'Red. A big buckle. Plastic. A big bag, looked as if it held a lot.'

But no large red bag appeared. Pirt, disgruntled by the failure of his men, was of the opinion that with so much impenetrable bush out there they had Buckley's of finding anything. He reminded Verdun and Briggs that when a small plane had crashed in the bush a couple of years back it had taken the searchers a full day to find it. He closed the door a mite loudly. 'A handbag!' he muttered, unconsciously mimicking Wilde's Lady Bracknell. 'Needle in a 'aystack!'

Nick Verdun sat opposite Simon Lee and regarded him thoughtfully. 'I know these calls were made,' he said. 'I think that was what triggered off the whole dreadful thing. Your phone number was on the list, so I assume that she also called you. What was it about?'

Lee stared at the floor. His naturally reserved nature found it hard to allow anyone (even a policeman as sensitively aware as Verdun) into the private side of his life. He took a deep breath, looking up into the sharply focussed gaze of the detective.

'It was nothing much. She had discovered something about my—my daughter. I told her to mind her own business. She said that morals *were* her business, that it was time the leading people in the town were brought to task. I told her that if she tried to approach me again with matters that were no concern of hers I would call the police.' He gave a sad, gentle smile. 'She laughed, then slammed down the phone. I was very angry.'

'Your daughter?'

'Yes. I was married once. My wife left me, many years ago. We had one daughter, who later…' He frowned, clearly moved. 'Do you need to know, Sergeant?'

'It'll go no further. And it would help.'

'She went with my wife—she was about fifteen at the time. She didn't want to stay with me—perfectly natural, a girl should be with her mother. Then she began to hang around the Cross— King's Cross, you know. I suppose I should be honest about it and say she—went on the streets. Later I heard that she had died of an overdose of some drug or other.' His hands were clasped tightly together, and he stared down at them. 'My wife didn't think to tell me at the time. I only heard weeks later…'

Verdun felt deeply sorry for the man. The façade of anxious amiability clearly held a confusion of agonies. 'Who could have known about this?'

'Several people knew when Lois left me. And when I heard of Katie's death I—well, I broke down for a while. So there would be perhaps a dozen or so people still in the town who would remember that I had had a tragedy in my life, though perhaps not the exact details. They were very kind to me. I had no sense of anyone withdrawing from me, then or later.'

'So Miss Glencosset could have picked up the story quite innocently and then used it to try to frighten you.' Verdun sat, thinking. 'Did she make any kind of threat?'

'No. I didn't quite understand why the information had any importance for her. She couldn't blackmail me, because there were people who already knew a lot about it. She couldn't make me dance to whatever tune she was playing, because what she knew of me didn't matter anymore. She could only hurt me…'

'I believe that may have been what she was after. Simply knowing what lay behind the serene front most of us wear. Knowing, and using it to upset people. Had she tried it on before?'

'Once or twice.' Simon Lee frowned. 'Was she mad? Was that it?'

'What is madness? She certainly wasn't well balanced. And she quite certainly had a mean and nasty streak in her. But it hardly adds up into murder, does it?' Verdun took out his notebook. 'Do these initials mean anything to you?' He turned to the right page. 'RW? EY? YE? NT?' Lee was shaking his head at each one. 'RN? ST? EO? NE? LI? OY?'

'Are they names, do you think?'

'Yes, I believe so. Names, or some other means of recognition. But they don't seem to link up with anyone in the area.'

'Where did you find them?'

Verdun hesitated. Surely it could do no harm to tell him? 'Miss Glencosset kept a very comprehensive diary. These initials reappear, page after page. But she was so very carefully obscure in her references that it's difficult to pin anything down. It's not in shorthand, but it might as well be.' He put the notebook away. 'If I could crack that particular code I think the whole thing might fall into place. Though Natalie's death complicates matters more than a little.' He stood. 'Thank you for your time. I needn't say, need I, that what we have discussed must go no further?'

Lee inclined his head gravely. 'I feel honoured that you have shown such trust in me, Sergeant. It will not be betrayed.'

Outside, Verdun stood for a moment. A nice old bloke, Simon Lee. He hoped he was out of the running. If they could locate the entry that would throw light on Lee's sad story, it would be another step forward.

Within the house, Simon stood before a photograph of his wife and the daughter he had loved; he felt a surge of the old anger and frustration and then, surprisingly, relief.

Stephen Harcourt mopped his brow, trying not to let Sylvia, who was watching him surreptitiously through the office window, see that he was upset. Nick Verdun's visit had taken him by surprise, though he realised that he should have expected it. But with one thing and another, and above all the worry about certain carefully obscured development details that seemed as if they might be getting out of hand, he had almost successfully shelved his concern over Glencosset and young Natalie. A man could stand only so much.

What had he given away to the eagle-eyed sergeant? He had almost forgotten that phone call, though at the time it seemed to block out everything else. The old bat had known too much! Where had she found her information? From someone on the council, or more deviously in some way he couldn't quite ascertain, through the bank or...? He mopped again. She'd had a source of information, anyway, and she'd used it.

Stephen recalled the anger he'd felt as that voice had levelled accusations at him. If he had had her in front of him he wouldn't have answered for the consequences. The deal was so near completion, so fragile, so carefully nursed into being, that the very thought of the whole thing falling down around his ears was more than he could bear.

Had Verdun believed him when he said she had simply been asking him for advice about a property she wanted to buy? 'Why had she wanted to buy a property?' he had asked. 'Was she thinking of leaving the school?'

No, not that he had known, Stephen had replied. 'Perhaps for her retirement. It couldn't be that far away.'

'Where did she want to buy it? Here, in town?'

Stephen had hedged. 'She wasn't specific. We agreed to meet sometime—when Mikado was over,' he said with a stroke of imagination. Then he frowned at Verdun. 'How did you know she had rung me?'

'She left a list,' the detective said laconically. 'She had quite a session of phone calls that afternoon.' He had taken out that damned notebook. '"*Advice on purchase of property*",' he said aloud as he wrote it down, glancing up at Harcourt in a manner that clearly took leave to doubt his veracity. That was when Stephen started to sweat.

Now he leaned back in his chair and called Sylvia to bring him a cup of coffee. 'Everything all right?' she asked solicitously, worried by the traces of perspiration, the general demeanour. She liked her boss to be in control; any variation in mood affected her as some are affected by the weather.

'Quite all right,' he said, slightly irritated. He wished she would go away.

'Everything OK with the policeman?'

'Everything perfectly OK!' Do stop fussing, girl!'

Sylvia drew herself up. She wouldn't let him see how much it hurt her when he was sharp. He watched her offended back leave the office, and sighed. Women! What was he to do? The other woman (Mary, who never fussed or irritated him) would have to be kept out of this. For the first time he wished he had steered clear of the complications of shonky dealings. It had seemed a good idea, when he had started a couple of years ago, learning the ropes by trial and error. It had seemed a magnificent idea when, after laying the groundwork with meticulous care, he found that it was actually possible to make a very great deal of money from taking only a tiny step over the edge of propriety.

Now, perhaps, he was going to see the whole carefully balanced edifice come tumbling down—and all because of that dreadful woman whose death nobody could possibly mourn. He tried to forget Natalie Percy, who had not deserved to die.

Diaries? Verdun had mentioned diaries. He put down his coffee, losing the taste for it. If it was all in the diaries, then why had Verdun asked him? Why hadn't he just run him in? For a moment he grew a little more hopeful; perhaps he had been bluffing. But in that case—how had he known about the phone call?

Sylvia Milton, quite unable to work while her boss was so distrait, yearned to be allowed to take some of the weight from his shoulders, but feared being rebuffed. She pecked at her typewriter, and was alarmed to see that she had started a letter, *'Darling Sir...'*

21

Nick Verdun and Briggs sat at Pirt's desk with identical lists before them. On one piece of paper was the collection of initials; on the other the names of likely suspects. Briggs was letting his eyes run up and down them, looking for any clue they might have missed.

In addition, on Verdun's side of the desk was a brief resumé of such details as Miss Glencosset's diaries had yielded up, and in particular those including the initials. 'Any ideas?' he said, glancing across at Briggs, who shook his head. For a while they were silent, deep in thought. 'Well,' he said at last, 'I've been to see all the phone numbers on that list, and they are all as innocent as the day they were born.'

He referred to his notes again. 'The Reverend Charles says he doesn't properly recall! Naturally. His kingdom, as they say, is not of this world. Young Mr Shafto, while sweating copiously, assured me that she had asked him to get her a new cheque book. We can *check* that!' He grinned. 'We have to take our fun where we can these days, Briggs.'

'Fun, sir—or pun?' Briggs retorted, slowly coming back to normal after his deep mood of despair.

'Kowalski the butcher says she wanted to order meat. When I asked if that was normal, he hedged a bit and said "not normal, but not unheard of". I wondered why anyone whose catering was done for her should order meat. When I asked him what the order was he couldn't recall. When I suggested he might have written it down he went red and mumbled. Either he's guilty of something, or he's totally inefficient.'

Briggs gave half a grin. 'Kowalski can't think of much else than the seductive Molly de Vance.'

'Is that so? Not a very promising liaison, I should have thought. Talking of whom, it seems Miss Glencosset rang *her* to tell her to mend her ways regarding the sexual purity of the local men.'

Briggs raised his eyebrows. 'Did she say that?'

'Not exactly. She said, "The old hag told me to stop chucking myself at the fellers"!'

'And what did the fair Molly say in reply?'

'She didn't say. But I gather it was an ear-piece full. She wasn't taking that from the old...' He searched his notes. 'I don't seem to have recorded her descriptive abilities.'

'What about Spenlow?'

'Yes—Spenlow. He assures me that no one rang that afternoon. Seemed quite surprised that I should think he and La Glencosset were on chatting terms. His wife was out, so I can only assume that, as the lady rang everyone else, she would also have rung Jasper.' He regarded his notes thoughtfully, dropping the light facetiousness. 'Natalie's number was on the list. But she was at work, and perhaps that was one call that didn't get made.'

'Why should she ring Natalie?'

'I don't know. Did she have a hold over her, too?' He rubbed his hand through his hair, brain-weary. 'Did she have a hold on anyone?'

'She had one, or thought she had, on Simon Lee.'

'I know. But how does it all hang together? How far back do we have to go? And is the danger now over? That's what really bothers me.' He yawned suddenly. 'Check out the phone records. We need to find Spenlow's number there, and the length of the call.'

It was an entry in a diary nearly ten years old that finally rendered up a clue. Frustrated, angered, alarmed by his inability to get to the bottom of what should have been a simple problem of detection, Nick Verdun had gone back in time and arrived at a passage that had not yet been cloaked in Teresa Glencosset's enigmatic style.

'Had a session with the tearful Miss P. These silly girls! Getting themselves into all kinds of trouble with quite unsuitable men. Now she thinks I can help her to escape her just deserts.'

Verdun read on, skipping pages until he arrived at another entry towards the end of the year. *'Miss P now fully aware of the consequences of wrong-doing. Baby taken for adoption. Shall make sure that Miss P does not stray again from straight and narrow. A useful child, but foolish. She knows what the score is.'*

With the book open before him, Verdun let his eyes wander around this supremely respectable room. If anyone now knew the 'consequences of wrong-doing', it was surely Miss Glencosset herself, removed from life because she kept a finger in every pie. 'Miss P.' Who was she? Where did she fit in? He wished with passion that just once the murdered woman had made a plain statement in these infuriating books.

An idea came to him out of nowhere. Suppose they were *all* in it? An unusual example of team work. Was there anything in that?

'Suppose,' he said later to Briggs, 'that "Miss P" was Natalie Percy?'

'Why her?' demanded Briggs, ready to defend the girl's reputation.

'Because she knew Glencosset ten years ago. She was a student at St Chedwyn's.' He had another thought. 'Go to the school and ask Mrs Parker if there are any records of attendance for that year. Find out if Natalie had an unexplained absence for, say, six or seven months.'

'It doesn't prove anything if she did.'

'It'll be a pointer,' Verdun said firmly. 'You wanted to be on the case—get going!'

'What are you going to do?'

Nick Verdun looked up at him, another idea striking. Three ideas within a very short space of time! 'I'm going to have a word with Corinne Lambert.' He grinned. 'You were so busy with Natalie that you took no notice of Corinne. Another pretty maid! She was about Natalie's age, and she's kept a very low profile. Of all the members of the G and S, she is the one who has never shown her face. We'll see what she knows about "Miss P".'

Corinne was startled to see the detective. She opened the door to him with a noticeable lack of enthusiasm, glancing behind her to the kitchen, where someone, perhaps her mother, was doing some fairly noisy baking.

'I'd like to talk to you about Natalie Percy.' Verdun slid himself inside with professional cunning.

Corinne indicated a chair and sat herself opposite to him, knees close together, hands clasped around them. 'Very self-protective,' Verdun noted. 'Nervous, too.'

'I didn't know her so well recently,' she began. 'Not like when we were kids.'

'It's not recently that I'm interested in,' Verdun said, smiling reassuringly. He was intrigued to see that a flicker crossed her face.

'What then?'

'I need to know what happened ten years ago,' he said bluntly. Corinne's face flushed. She was clearly disturbed.

'I don't know what you mean.'

Suddenly, as sometimes happened to him, Verdun knew he was on the edge of something that would turn his investigation right round. Corinne knew what he was talking about—he would have laid bets on it. 'Her pregnancy,' he said; and Corinne, taking a quick breath of surprise, gave him an astonished glance from eyes full of anxiety.

'I don't...' she began, but he cut in.

'Yes, you do!' He leaned forward. 'Apart from the fact that if you have information the law requires you to pass it on, there is that other nasty fact—someone out there has killed twice. I see no reason why he shouldn't kill again—do you?' he gave her his most encouraging smile. 'I'm not psychic, Corinne. I have to work on evidence, on proof. *I have to know!* You hold in your memory some things which will help me to wind the case up and leave this town safe and ready to go on with its normal life. You *have* to give me that information.'

He watched as she struggled with herself. At last she sighed. 'Well, she's dead now. I suppose that absolves me.'

'She made you swear not to tell?'

'Yes. She wasn't supposed to tell anyone else.'

'Who made her promise? Miss Glencosset?'

'Yes. But just before she went away she told me all about it. Well, nearly all. She wouldn't tell me who the father was, except that he had been in town for a short while and then moved on.' She bit her lips, and Verdun saw she was near to tears. 'She was only fifteen, and I don't think she really knew what was happening to her—not until he had gone. She was crazy about him, I know that.'

'So she went to Miss Glencosset?' Corinne nodded. 'Why?'

'Natalie had no family. She lived with a sort of cousin. She didn't want to tell her—they didn't get on too well. And Miss Glencosset found her in the school loo one day and sort of guessed what was the matter.'

'She was very angry?'

'No. Funnily enough. She told Natalie that she mustn't speak about it to anyone else, and that she would look after her. And she did. Natalie was packed off to somewhere in the country, and after the baby was born she gave it up for adoption. Then she came back here, and back to school, and Miss Glencosset accepted her without fees.'

'What did the "sort of cousin" say about this?'

'Miss Glencosset went to see her and told her that the school doctor had diagnosed TB. The cousin made no fuss at all when she knew that Miss Glencosset was paying all the bills.'

'Didn't that strike anyone as strange?'

'*I* thought it was pretty off. I didn't know what she hoped to get out of it. I thought perhaps...' Corinne stopped, confused.

'You thought perhaps she had a sexual interest in Natalie?' The girl nodded. 'But it wasn't that?'

'No. It was odd, really. It was more as though she liked having power over Nat. If Nat didn't toe the line, Miss G would spill the beans. That kind of thing.'

'And would that have mattered? In these days?'

'In this town? Yes! Natalie was a very sensitive person. Besides...' She stopped abruptly.

'Besides—it didn't stop there, did it?' Verdun regarded her with sympathy. 'You were pretty good friends, weren't you?'

'Yes, we were. We clicked somehow. So she told me things when she couldn't bear it anymore.'

'Why didn't you tell me all this before?'

'It was Natalie's secret. She had a good reason for killing the old...Miss G. Then, when someone killed Nat, it seemed too late.'

'If she *had* been the killer, what would you have done?'

Corinne gazed past him, her eyes bright with tears. 'Gone on being her friend, if she wanted. She was pushed to it.'

'Do you still think she did it?'

'No. Not since she was killed. Doesn't make sense.'

'So what does make sense?'

'Miss Glencosset had tabs on lots of people. Anyone could have done it.'

'Was this generally known?'

'I don't think so. I knew it because Nat told me bits, now and again.'

Verdun regarded her thoughtfully. 'Corinne, do *you* know who these people are? Do you know what their secrets are? Did she tell you that?'

'No.' Corinne shook her head wearily. 'She never said. She kept it to herself. Just things like "she's on the warpath again—got her claws in"!'

'But the fire was sometimes fed by Natalie's information? Where did she get it?'

Corinne almost smiled. 'You know small towns. Hot-beds of intrigue! If you really make the effort you can pick up a lot without much difficulty.'

Verdun was puzzled. 'But didn't Natalie ever try to break free? She'd had a good education, yet she was still in the supermarket...'

The girl's face tightened. 'No! She wasn't particularly well-educated. Not enough to get a really good job. Oh, she went to school, but what happened to her just about broke her up. It was years before...'

He could sense she was on the edge of refusing to answer any more questions.

'Why didn't she tell Miss G to get stuffed?'

'Because—because Miss Glencosset knew where the child was. And Natalie was afraid of what she would do. I think—I think it may have been an illegal adoption. No papers, you see.' She closed her eyes and tears began to squeeze through. 'She was a rotten, dreadful woman, Mr Verdun. Thank God she's gone!'

'What a pity Natalie didn't tell me all this.' She nodded without speaking. Verdun stood and went to the door. The kitchen was still producing sounds like the smashing of pots, but neither of them was aware of it. 'She might have been saved.'

'Don't you think I know that? I told her she should...' She gave a sob. 'I told her...'

Verdun watched her with compassion. 'You were *always* very good friends, weren't you?' Corinne nodded. 'Why did you say you weren't?'

'I was scared,' the girl admitted. 'I was trying to distance myself. You don't know what it's been like.'

The detective nodded soothingly. 'It'll all be over soon,' he promised. 'Meanwhile, I'd like you to go away somewhere, just for a short while, until we get it sorted out.' She stared up at him. 'Natalie was probably killed because she was seen talking to my young fellow Briggs. Can you get away?'

'You mean someone might want to...? Oh, that's terrible!' She thought quickly. 'Yes, I can go to someone.' She stood, gazing at him with urgency. 'Who is it, do you know?'

'No, not yet. But soon. And when it's completed you can come home and pick up the threads and forget all about it.'

Corinne laughed, short and hard. 'Forget? That's what you think. I shall never forget!'

'You'd be surprised how soon things will return to normal.'

She shook her head. 'But Natalie won't be here.'

Verdun, suddenly grim, went out and closed the door behind him.

22

Molly de Vance swung her way along the main street. It was the sort of day that always brought out the best in her: that is, it made her feel full of affection towards her fellow men. She crossed the road so that she could pass Michael Kowalski's shop, and tapped on his window while he was serving a customer. His beefy face turned a little redder.

When the shop was empty she went in, slinking her way up to the counter in a manner she had long perfected. 'Hi, Mike!' she said in languorous tones, and he, much alarmed, glanced about him quickly as if searching for somewhere to hide.

'What you doing here?' he asked, perhaps more belligerently than he had intended, for the sight of her made butterflies flutter in his chest and elsewhere. 'I told you...'

'Friends, Mike. We're friends, aren't we? I can call to see my friends.'

'In this shop and this apron I'm a butcher,' he declared. 'A butcher don't have no friends. He has customers. What can I sell you?' His placed his fists wide apart on the counter, and fixed her with a ferocious scowl.

'My! We are tough today.' She leaned against the counter on her own side and laughed up into his face. 'Different from last time, eh?'

'I don't want to hear about that, thanks. That was an error of judgement, and I don't wish to discuss it.' There was considerable dignity in him.

But Molly laughed again, that sharp-as-crystal laugh that he had once found enchanting. 'Right old sheep's head you are, Mike Kowalski! Don't you worry about me, mate. I'm off to Singapore at the end of next week. Time I had a little holiday. Want to come with me?' At the expression on his face she laughed once more, loud and mocking, and he pulled himself away from the counter and busied himself at the back of the shop, waiting there until he heard the door shut. Then, his body riven by strangely opposing sensations—was it love or hate he felt?—he took up his cleaver and ruined a perfectly good lamb's carcase. But it was worth it.

Molly, meanwhile, smiling at what she considered a victory over one of nature's fools, continued on her way. She passed the hotel where Verdun and Briggs were staying, the police station where Pirt was at that moment making a pot of blackest tea, which Verdun would drink rather than offend, and Briggs would pour into the lavatory; and fate or fortune led her into the path of the Rev Charles Culbert, who had just been to the library.

For a dreadful moment of indecision he wondered if he could pretend he hadn't seen her; but there she was, right in front of him, and she was, after all, one of his flock (if only in theory); and when all was said and done he was man enough not to want to seem a complete fool in front of her.

'Good day,' he said, making a small bob of a bow; Molly, whose instincts worked very fast, glanced up at him through her eyelashes and returned the greeting. Then, to his alarm, she turned and fell into step beside him.

'Haven't seen you for days, Vicar,' she said, somehow giving him the feeling that he was cuddling her, though in fact there was a measurable gap between them. 'What have you been doing with yourself?'

'Oh, it's a busy time of the year,' he said, wondering how to escape; for since Kowalski had spilt the beans about the—the *substance*, he had been having very ambivalent thoughts about the gorgeous Molly. What should he do? What was his pastoral duty to her, his civic duty to the police, his moral duty to those who would be dragged into disgrace by the *substance* she was reputed to import? And then, was it even true? Had Kowalski simply been trying to get back at her through spite? Had she rejected (oh, how painful the thought!) the butcher's advances, and so incurred his anger?

'Busy? How, busy? What does a vicar have to do?'

'Well, there's a lot of visiting,' he began.

'You never visit me!' she replied quickly, smiling up at him. 'Why don't you visit me, Vicar? I'm a very deserving case.'

Oh, heavens! She was mocking him. She was mocking his shepherding of the flock. He stumbled a little, his feet the last thing on his mind. 'Upsy-daisy!' Molly said, taking his arm as if he was in his dotage.

'I should, yes, of course, I should,' he heard himself saying, gabbling the words out. He couldn't remember when he had been more frightened. If he went to see her, she might offer him some of the *substance*—he might not be strong enough... 'Oh, Lord!' he prayed silently but with passionate fervour, 'Lead me not into temptation!'

It seemed to work, for Molly, coming level with the travel agency, stopped. 'I'm going to Singapore next week,' she said, making it sound like an invitation. 'Got to go and pay off my ticket. Nice talking to you. Ta-ta!' And, mercifully, he was on his own again.

He resisted the desire to glance around and see who had noticed the brief meeting; he had nothing to be ashamed of. But he did now have a mighty problem to solve: if she was off to Singapore, someone should warn the authorities. He didn't want it to be him, but he had a moral... 'Oh, to hell with morals!' he muttered, tripping over a badly placed paving stone. She had been laughing at him. She thought him a fool, less than a man, a comedy figure out of a bad play. And the worst of it was that he agreed with her.

So, if he told the police about her little jaunts (always supposing Kowalski's facts could be relied on) was he doing it to get his own back, or to perform his duty as a good citizen? The dilemma kept him busy all the way back to the rectory, when he realised that he had intended to buy some margarine for his afternoon slice of toast.

'Serves me right,' he said, standing in the kitchen, from which Mrs Bedwell had gone some time ago. 'Dry toast will make me remember that all sin must be paid for in the end.'

But it was not the stimulating comfort he had expected it to be.

23

Briggs, his youthful brow furrowed, went once again through the list of initials. It made no sense to have them sitting there, offering nothing; he and Verdun had searched through the local business directory and ratepayers' details at the local council offices; but no names had emerged that made any sense. Could the dead woman have had a whole list of victims outside the town? Unlikely. She seemed to have led a life contained within the boundaries of town, school and opera group.

It was infuriating. He was certain that he was looking at something that would contain the clue they needed to break through to a solution to the crimes.

He read the initials slowly once more, mouthing them to himself; and then he glanced at the list of suspects and others, written out in Verdun's careful hand. His eyes went back and forth between the two, and whether it was a sudden flash of inspiration or simply a new slant on the letters as they lay before him, suddenly he had the answer.

'They're not initials,' he said, looking up at his boss. 'They're the opposite.'

'What do you mean?'

'The old girl wanted a record of her victims, but names or initials would have been too obvious, if anyone had found the diaries. Or perhaps she just had the kind of mind that likes cryptic clues or anagrams. My mother,' he said, defying Verdun's frown, 'does crosswords. You have to be able to see words...'

'All right, all right!' Verdun said impatiently. 'So what is it I have been missing all this time?'

'They're the *last* letters of names. Look! Natalie Percy: EY! Chester Parkinson: RN. Jasper Spenlow: RW. It works!'

'It's daft!' Verdun exploded. 'It's childish, like those silly games we used to play as kids—gangs and codes and all that.'

'It kept *us* going, anyway.'

Nick Verdun pushed his chair back and rubbed his eyes. 'But then, of course, she *was* childish, Briggs. It's all been the spite-for-spite's-sake that you see in the school yard. "I'll tell on you, Mary Smith!" Childish! Perhaps she was in schools too long.' He frowned. 'Are you sure?' he asked, nervous of believing their luck.

'ST: Charles Culbert. EO: Dave Shafto. It seems to be working.'

'Who's YE?'

Briggs slid his eyes down their list. 'Could be Molly de Vance.'

'That would be YEE.'

'Well, maybe it's someone else. Does it help?'

'It has to. It means that I can link names with references, and so make the references more comprehensible.' He stood up stiffly. 'I still think it's infantile.' He turned and put a hand on the younger man's shoulder. 'Good work, Briggs. Excellent!'

'What's next?" Briggs, rightly pleased with himself, pushed the papers together and replaced them in their manila file.

'Make the rounds again, with a bit more hope of getting somewhere. Then...'

Pirt entered with a sideways jab of his head indicating there was someone to see the detectives. (Pirt was beginning to wonder if he would ever get his office back). Behind him, shrunken with apprehension, was Dave Shafto. 'Wants to have a word,' Pirt said, leaving and shutting the door firmly.

'Yes?' Verdun sat down and indicated a chair. Shafto, his face white with worry, sat on its extreme edge. 'What can I do for you?'

The young man was clearly wishing he had not come. He opened and shut his mouth several times before clearing his throat and beginning in a voice maddeningly out of control. 'There's something I've got to tell you.'

Nick Verdun regarded him with interest. 'Well, shoot away!'

After a long pause: 'I don't know how to start.'

'At the beginning,' Verdun suggested. 'What's it about?'

'I work at the bank,' Dave said miserably.

'Yes, I know.'

'I'm afraid I may have committed a crime.'

'Aren't you sure?'

'Well, I didn't mean to.' Verdun had nodded at Briggs to take notes, and Shafto half turned and watched him take the pen from his pocket. 'It was just a bit of silliness, but I didn't think they meant…'

'Right!' said the detective, putting a bit of backbone into the proceedings. 'Tell me exactly what you did.'

Dave Shafto sat up a little straighter. 'I had a couple of mates, used to go drinking with them down at the hotel. Known them for some time. One day we got talking. They asked me some things about the bank, about money and deliveries of cash and all that sort of thing. I hadn't been at the bank long, so it was all pretty new to me. I didn't mean anything bad by it—just shooting my mouth off, I reckon. Stupid, but it never dawned on me. But then the next time I saw them they'd sorta got the wrong idea. Thought I was going to do some kind of bust with them. I told them it was more than my job was worth. They said it was a piece of cake, that we'd split the dough between us. I told them "no", that I didn't want any part of it. But they wouldn't let go!' He stared from one man to the other. 'Honest, I never thought of anything like that. Just talking big, I reckon…You know…?'

Verdun nodded, his mind working fast. 'Why have you come to us now?'

'Because it's getting me down. If they do a bust I'm involved, aren't I? But I never meant...'

'Right! You can give all the details to Constable Briggs here, and then it won't be your responsibility anymore.'

'Do I have to give you their names?' Verdun nodded, and the young man shifted unhappily in his chair. 'I won't half think before I do anything as daft as this again.'

'Good. At least you'll be able to sleep at nights. Tell me,' Verdun said casually, 'did anyone else know about this?'

'Pattie Fisher. You know—Yum-Yum? She told me I was barmy and made me promise to come and see you.'

'Anyone else?'

There was a long pause before Shafto said, 'No.'

'Are you sure?" Verdun was watching him closely.

'Well, Miss Glencosset sorta guessed.'

'*Sorta* guessed? How could she?'

'I don't know.' The youngster looked thoroughly depressed now, and not a little scared.

'She rang you up, didn't she? But not for the cheque book. She rang you to tell you that she knew what you'd been up to. So who told her?'

'She was a nosey old woman!' Dave suddenly exploded. 'She always seemed to know things before people had even done them.'

'Somebody probably killed her for it,' Verdun said quietly, watching like a hawk. Shafto sat quite still for a moment, then turned so pale he looked on the point of fainting.

'Not me,' he said, his voice hoarse. 'You don't think it was me?'

'Probably not.' Verdun was not quite prepared to let him off the hook. 'But we have to consider every avenue.'

'I'd gone,' Shafto whispered. 'I couldn't have.'

'Natalie Percy heard your bike roar away. From what she told us you would have had time—just.'

'Natalie?' He stared from one to the other in burgeoning panic. 'Why Natalie? What's she got to do with it?'

'Natalie was a very observant young lady. She often saw things people would rather keep to themselves.'

'I don't understand. I don't understand any of it. Why did you ask Natalie about me?'

'It came up in her evidence.' Verdun stood, breaking the fragile mood. 'Do you have anything else to tell us?' Shafto, deeply anxious, moved slowly towards the door.

'I don't know anything but what I said—about the bank. And I'm sorry about that.' Briggs, notebook at the ready, ushered him out to make a proper statement, and Nick Verdun sank back into his chair and put his fingers together in a peak while he pondered on the latest developments.

The boy didn't do it, he was sure of that.

Well, he thought he was sure.

He had barely had time to go through the list of letters (what *was* the opposite of 'initial'? he wondered) when Pirt showed in another visitor.

'Good day, Vicar,' Verdun said as jovially as he could, faced with a cleric clearly carrying most of the world's troubles. 'How can I help you?'

'It is rather,' said Culbert lugubriously, 'how I can help you. At least, I come bearing information, though in fact I am not certain of its authenticity and would be more than happy should it be discovered that I have been misinformed. However, after much struggling with my spiritual self I have come to the conclusion that the decision is not mine, that there are others more qualified to make such a decision, and that in fact I have a wider duty to those I know within my own parish. A duty, in fact, to others who might well be affected, very seriously affected, if I do not speak out. Though, as you can understand...'

'Hold on, sir! Hold on. I don't have the slightest idea what you're talking about.'

This direct approach stopped Culbert in his tracks, but brought into his face such a look of distress that, for a moment, Verdun wondered if he was about to reveal the murderer. Surely nothing less horrendous than murder could put such a pallor on the cheek? For a moment abject fear peered out of the eyes of the man of God, and then, slowly, the mourning expression crept back and, with a deep breath to sustain him, Culbert began to speak. And this time Verdun understood what he was saying.

'We do not, to my knowledge, have a drug problem in this town, Mr Verdun. But it has recently come to my ears that there is a member of our community who—ah—uses certain substances, and who brings them in from those areas of south-east Asia in which they are easily found. I have been much disturbed by the fact. I am not a very worldly man, Sergeant, but this seems to me to be a thing which is most undesirable, especially where there are young people.'

'Are you going to tell me who it is, Mr Culbert?'

The vicar straightened in his chair, putting his head a little on one side as he contemplated the question. 'No,' he said at last. 'I have brought the matter to your notice. It is up to you now.' He hesitated briefly. 'If one of our neighbours were to take a trip to—ah—Singapore within a short time from now, it might well be to your advantage to make enquiries.' He closed his mouth in a symbolic movement, then opened it again to say, 'That is all. Thank you, Sergeant Verdun. I have nothing more to say.'

'But I have, sir! I'll pass on your information to the proper authorities. But I want to ask you one question. When I suggested that Miss Glencosset had rung you on the afternoon of her death, you agreed, but said that you couldn't recall what it was about. I'll ask you again. What did she say to you?'

The Rev Mr Culbert lowered his gaze to the floor and a look of calm martyrdom crossed his pale face. He sighed. 'In my job, Sergeant, one is very vulnerable. Sometimes it is elderly spinster ladies who conceive a great passion for one, sometimes it is a clash of wills where a gentleman of the congregation resents one's apparent authority. Miss Glencosset, who had, I fear, a rather spiteful nature, had it firmly in her mind that a man of my age and solitary state would be quite unable to resist the charms of the choirboys.' He glanced up with a small, patient smile on his face.

'There was no foundation for this. I am not a very physical man at any time, but if I were my inclination would not be towards young boys. Miss Glencosset simply did not believe me. That's all!'

Verdun nodded slowly, sympathetically. 'And she plagued you with this?'

'Oh—plagued? She rang, now and then, to enquire how I was getting on. She was a sadly disappointed woman herself, I imagine. I found it disturbing, of course, and annoying—but not to the extent of deciding to kill her!' His smile was stronger, his mood noticeably lighter. Then the mood went. 'As for the iniquity of killing that poor girl Natalie...'

'Yes,' Verdun agreed. 'There has been wickedness abroad in this pleasant town.'

'Solve it, Mr Verdun, and give us back our peace.'

They stood, and Verdun held out his hand. 'Thank you, sir, for coming. We're doing our best. I think—we may be within sight of a solution.'

After the vicar had gone, Verdun sat alone, staring into space. He recognised the sensation of being at the far end of a long tunnel, engulfed in darkness, the light so far away as to be no more than a star on a cloudy night. But it did seem as if the star had begun to twinkle.

24

Simon Lee, in the act of locking up for the night, saw the headlights of a car swing into his driveway and peered through the curtains to see who was honouring him at this hour.

The knock at the door was peremptory, and he took a quick peep through the porch window, a little nervous so late at night. He glanced at the clock—just short of eleven. He opened the door to reveal the Parkinsons, huddled together as if they were cold. 'Come in!' he cried, more than a little alarmed at the unexpectedness of the visit.

They stood in his lounge room, hand in hand like children, and Simon sensed that Bella was in charge, that for some reason Chester had lost his belligerent pose and was thankful to hold his wife's hand as a protection. Against what?

'A drink?' He was unsure what to do with them, standing there unspeaking, neither apparently prepared to make the first move. Chester began to nod, but Bella said 'no' in a firm voice. 'Then sit down, sit down,' he begged them, taking a chair himself, and they placed themselves carefully on the sofa, still holding hands, still staring at him as if it was his idea that they should come. 'Now, how can I help you?'

'We have some unpleasant news, Simon,' Bella said in a low voice. ('They've discovered the murderer,' was his immediate thought). 'I have asked Chester to come and tell you about it, so that you can decide what is to be done.' She turned to her husband, and a look of pure affection suffused her face. As if she talked to a child, she said, 'Go on, my dear. Simon's listening'.

Chester, his eyes on the floor, told the story of his foolishness. How he had been unable to stop the business going downhill, had tried to borrow from the bank, but without success, had eventually turned to the only ready money available to him.

'I have taken money from the G and S account,' he said finally, lifting his gaze painfully to that of his president, whose own eyes were full of compassion. 'I have taken five thousand dollars, a little at a time, to pay pressing accounts. That is the society's renovation fund, plus the additional money raised by the car-park sales throughout the year. And I have no means of paying it back.' He put a hand to his face, where a nerve was twitching. 'We shall have to sell, if we can find a buyer. Then, I hope, I can replace what I have taken. Meanwhile, I throw myself on your kindness, Simon, and beg forgiveness.'

'My dear fellow!' Simon leaned across from his chair, hands outstretched, and took Chester's cold hands in them. 'My dear man, you have been going through purgatory. And I didn't know! I am much to blame—yes, I am! I should have been more meticulous as president—I should have seen, as your friend, that you were troubled.' He stood up and went to a cabinet in the corner of the room. 'You are to have something to drink! Both of you! You are shocked and cold and unhappy. What are friends for,' he cried, 'if not to bear each other's burdens?' He handed them their glasses with a touch of ceremony.

'Now, my dear Chester, you are not to think about this sad business for a another moment. We will go through the books and I will make up the deficit until such time as you can repay. About your shop,' he said, his face lengthening, 'I can do little, I'm afraid.

But we can at least see that your other worry is obliterated from your mind. Drink up!' he cried again, as if this were a party of celebration.

Bella, her eyes full, came to him and embraced him warmly, kissing him on the cheek and holding him to her fine bosom. Simon felt the heat rising in his face. This was a most stimulating meeting, a time to show solidarity and strength. He beamed on Bella and Chester as if they had given him some great gift.

'You are a gentleman!' Chester said, overwhelmed. 'We shall never forget your kindness.'

Simon looked down into his glass, his head a little tilted. 'When you are elderly and alone,' he said, 'few things ever happen unexpectedly. Life becomes planned to the last degree. People stop asking you to do things, because they don't want to bother you. It sometimes becomes very boring.' He chuckled. 'Perhaps that's why I enjoy Gilbert and Sullivan so much. It is my one trip into fantasy.' His face grew serious. 'I have been fortunate in the practical side of life, and now I have all the money I need for anything I may desire—and no one to share it with.' When he glanced up at them there was an impish smile on the pale face, and the oriental planes were emphasised. 'Thank you for giving me the opportunity to do something good with it.'

Chester, to his everlasting shame, gave a great hiccup and burst into tears.

25

'I am sick of police interviews,' Jasper said angrily. 'I am sick of that man Verdun. I am tired of saying the same thing over and over again. If they can't solve it they should put it down to experience and go away!'

'I'm not sure that they can,' Maggie said. 'At least this Verdun is a bit of a gentleman. Imagine if it had been left to Pirt!' She was pasting the latest newspaper review into her scrapbook.

'It'll drag on for ever,' Jasper fumed, and his wife glanced up at him.

'Why should you care?'

He paced irritably over to the window and stared out at a hibiscus that would benefit from some drastic pruning. 'It's unsettling.'

'Murder always is!' She grinned maliciously. 'Even Teresa Glencosset's. Never mind, you'll be back to work on Monday. That should take up the slack in your energy.'

He groaned. 'Bloody kids! I'm going to chuck it all up. They'll drive me mad.'

'My, my!' Maggie said in just the right tone of voice to add fuel to his fire. 'But what else can you do, Jasper darling? Who else, not to put too fine a point on it, would employ you?'

Jasper, jaw clenched, turned to stare at her. Uncharacteristically, he restrained himself from giving as good as he got. Instead he managed a tight, furious grin. 'Don't write me off, Maggie. Not yet! I may surprise you after all.'

Maggie mocked him. 'Promises, promises! What have *you* got up your sleeve?' And then, when he still refused to rise to her bait, 'Why *did* she ring you?'

He took a deep, infuriated breath. 'Not you too!' he said, and stormed out of the room.

Nick Verdun was finding that Jasper Spenlow's attitude was only an acute form of something that was beginning to afflict the whole town—or at least those citizens who qualified for inclusion on his list of suspects. It wasn't something that bothered him unduly; sometimes it was a positive benefit, because it meant that people's tempers were getting short, and their irritation with him and the system he represented not infrequently made them careless in their stories. Where these had been manufactured, the appearance of a crack in an otherwise perfect alibi could yield great rewards.

He had hoped for such a result from Jasper and Maggie during this most recent interview. But in spite of a lean and drawn look on the former's face and a flicker of wicked interest on Maggie's, there had been nothing. The diaries had simply stated: '*Today's the day! RW can watch out as Katisha goes into action.*' That was on the face of it a totally harmless comment on the day of a dress rehearsal. Only the fact that RW also appeared on the list of phone calls gave the entry an alternative meaning.

But Jasper had been adamant that no phone call had been received from Miss Glencosset that day. He had turned to Maggie for confirmation. 'We didn't hear from her, did we, darling?' And Maggie, glancing from one man to the other, had shaken her head.

'Jasper would have told me,' she said sweetly, with just a whiff of vinegar.

Verdun now knew they were lying; telephone records proved it. Jasper had been alone in the house; he *must* have taken the call. But he wouldn't be shaken.

The Parkinsons had puzzled him, too. Bella had a kind of regal splendour about her, a matriarchal glow that had dimmed Chester's stern husbanding into a flickering candle. Something quite radical had happened to them, he surmised. But when he asked, yet again, about that wretched phone call, an invisible wall had gone up, and all his shafts bounced off it.

'Indigestion mixture,' Chester said peevishly. 'I can't understand the fuss.'

Verdun, a flutter of hope in his breast, turned the pages of the ubiquitous notebook. 'Cough mixture, I think,' he said. Chester waved an irritable hand.

'Cough? Indigestion? What does it matter?' But there was a sliding away in his eyes, as if he preferred not to meet Verdun face to face.

'Everything and anything matters in a murder investigation, sir,' the detective said courteously. 'Was it cough mixture or indigestion mixture?' Gentle pressure—don't hurry him. 'I presume you could look it up?'

'If you really think it's important,' Chester said, almost rudely. Bella watched him, her hands held loosely in her lap; but her eyes were those of the mother who sees her child in danger.

Suddenly she spoke. 'Sergeant, is my husband under suspicion?' Chester, alarmed, flung his head up, trying to warn her. But she ignored him. 'This phone call, does it really matter?'

Nick Verdun turned towards her, approval in his expression. 'Miss Glencosset rang a number of people on that last afternoon, Mrs Parkinson. I believe that what was said is important to my investigation.'

She regarded him thoughtfully. 'Do you actually *know* who did it? Are you looking for corroboration? If my husband tells you, will that help?'

Verdun smiled. 'No, I don't actually know. Yes, I am looking for proof. And yes, if Mr Parkinson will tell me...'

'Tell him,' Bella said to Chester, nodding reassuringly. '*We* know that you're not involved. Everything will be all right.'

Chester, ashamed and broken, opened his mouth to reject her crazy notion; then suddenly realised what a relief it would be to have the burden taken off his back.

'Miss Glencosset rang to let me know that she had information...' He swallowed, his mouth dry. Verdun kept very quiet. 'I have been—taking money from the G and S, Sergeant. My business is failing. I was desperate. So I 'borrowed'—as you recall, I am—was—the treasurer.'

'Will charges be laid against you?'

'No. Simon Lee has behaved as the gentleman he is and given me time to pay it back. In fact, he has covered for me, and if it goes no further...'

'If it is not going to court, then I have no interest in it, Mr Parkinson. I shan't even make a note about it. All I needed was to know why the dead woman rang you.' He stood, nodding at them. 'Thank you.' Then he frowned. 'How do you suppose she knew? Had she seen the books?'

Parkinson shrugged. The colour had come back into his face. 'I can't imagine. A teller—someone at the bank? She was a prize sticky-beak. She always seemed to know everything about everybody. A menace, really. Not much liked.'

Bella, without losing her serenity, gave Verdun to understand that that went for her, too. Then her sense of fair play asserted itself. 'Though I must admit she was quite splendid on stage. A loss to the society.' She smiled gently. 'And yet we shall manage without her.'

'I do hope you will come to the barbecue at the weekend,' Bella had said to Verdun as he was leaving, and he had mumbled something trite about pressure of work and not his scene; but she had smiled at him and said that they all hoped he and his young officer would attend.

He doubted whether her feelings would be shared by other members whom he had had to revisit a number of times. But when the day dawned bright and Briggs, now recovering from his bruised susceptibilities, thought it might be a beaut idea, he relented, and they strolled slowly through the town and out to the park where the gas barbies were already burning nicely and a sizzle of steaks and sausages hit the nasal senses.

Apart from one or two who looked at them askance, there was little sense of their being unwelcome. Someone found them plates, salad appeared, and barbecue sauce and paper napkins; and Briggs wandered away to where the younger members were sitting on a jarrah log doing service as a seat.

Simon Lee came over to Verdun, greeting him with his usual courtesy. As they battled with the steaks (Verdun had often wondered why barbecue food, probably the most difficult to eat with any grace, had found itself into polite society—the only way to deal with it was to lie on the floor with the meat between one's paws and tear it apart), they chatted lightly of this and that. Then Lee said, 'Are you any nearer?' and Verdun nodded and said, 'Nearly there.'

Lee sighed. 'We're caught in a trap. Solving the murders will be such a relief—but how shall we react when one of our number is taken from us under such circumstances?'

Verdun agreed it was a tough one. He waved his fork around. 'A good turn-out.'

'A hundred percent, barring obvious absentees.'

'Would Miss Glencosset have come?'

'Oh, yes. She would have been in charge of something, undoubtedly. She was a leader, not a follower. I don't think she would ever have missed the chance of laying down the law.' He grinned wryly, a little ashamed of his own analysis.

Maggie joined them, balancing her plate with an ease that Verdun could only envy, as he dropped his bread roll for the third time. 'You managed to get some time off, then, Sergeant?' she said, making the simple question sound barbed. Tactfully, Lee wandered away.

Nick wondered whether to say that he was still on duty, but then held back. Perhaps a more laid-back attitude would bring something forth. 'Jack isn't always a dull boy,' he said, giving her the full force of his best smile. She regarded him with interest.

'You're quite couth for a policeman. I was saying to Jasper, thank God we aren't being investigated by old Pirt, who is a treasure when it comes to handing out speeding tickets or locating lost bicycles, but not quite your needle-sharp detective.'

Verdun decided to treat that as a compliment. 'I went to a good school,' he said lightly.

'You must know quite a bit about us now,' she went on, and he realised he was being pumped for information. 'Odd, really, to be able to go into a community like ours and ask all sorts of highly personal questions. I can think of a good few old biddies in this town who would be quite good at that.'

'Committing a criminal act rather opens the door on it, doesn't it? I can ask you anything that may have a bearing on the crime, but privacy is still important. I have to be very careful.'

'Let me ask *you* something,' she said, lowering her lids and gazing thoughtfully at him. 'Do you enjoy your work?'

There was a barb in there somewhere. He grinned at her. 'Yes, I do. I think it's important. Where would you be without us?'

She sighed, and bit off a piece of sausage, letting her eyes wander around the groups under the trees or gathered round the barbecues. 'Well,' she said at last, 'I can tell you it won't be my Jasper, anyway. He might have the idea, but he'd never carry it out.' She smiled serenely at him. 'But then, I'm sure all wives would say the same.'

'What a wife says about her husband isn't really evidence.' He adopted her bantering tone.

'Well, look at us!' she said, suddenly exasperated. 'Do we *look* like murderers?'

'That,' he retorted, 'is the problem.' She glanced at him quickly. 'It would be so much easier if criminals carried a kind of birthmark on them.'

'The mark of Cain? You'd be out of a job.'

He conceded the point. 'What seems strange to us, coming from outside, is how a peaceful little place like this could hold such passions that someone would kill to escape them. Not my idea of country living.'

'Oh, the country! We don't grow the glossy skin they have in the cities. The passions are probably nearer the surface.'

'So a Miss Glencosset comes into the place, and over the years stirs up so much anger in someone that tragedy follows.'

'She'd always been a bit that way,' Maggie said casually. 'I remember Jasper telling me…'

Nick Verdun felt something in his chest give a mighty lurch. Did she realise what she'd said? He nodded as if he knew what she was talking about. 'He knew her, of course.'

'I'm sure he told you.' She was suddenly alarmed.

'Yes.' He met her gaze with wide-eyed innocence. 'Though I don't know where they met.' He held his breath.

Maggie hesitated briefly. 'At college. He said they hardly knew each other—it was a huge campus. But he recognised her when she took the job at St Chedwyn's. Said she would take some handling, that she was a born stirrer.'

'Well,' Verdun said, his smile stuck to his face like a band aid, 'he wasn't wrong, was he?' He put his plate down on a picnic table. 'Can I get you another drink?'

She shook her head and watched him as he moved away. Had she imagined that he had tensed, ever so slightly, when she had mentioned those college days? But he was wandering round the picnic place, chatting to people, being charm itself, annoying no one. After a while she relaxed. When Jasper joined her they sat together on a park bench with a wine cask and a couple of glasses. 'You had a good chat with the fuzz,' Jasper said. 'What was he after?'

'Just having a pleasant day off.' But she was still not sure. 'Did you tell him you knew Teresa before, when you were young?'

He turned towards her, his brows fiercely creased. 'No. Why?'

'He seemed to know.' ('Or did I tell him?' she wondered.)

'Bloody interfering public nuisance!' he muttered, folding a fist and beating it on his thigh.

Maggie smiled sweetly at a passing couple, and laid her hand on his knee. 'The mask's slipping, darling,' she murmured. 'People will say we're *not* in love.'

'People,' he said with suppressed fury, looking across to where Verdun was talking to a young member of the chorus, 'can say what they damn well please! And *he* can go to hell!'

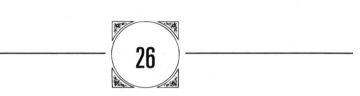

26

The Harcourts had arrived late. Stephen was looking darkly angry, Mary had a 'Patience on a monument' air about her. 'Hullo!' someone murmured as they crossed the leaf-strewn clearing, already filled with wisps of smoke. 'Stephen got out of bed the wrong side today!'

His mood had been brought on by another brush with the angry Mr Hailey, and for a moment he had seriously considered calling in the police to deal with the man when a load of animal feed had been dumped on his lawn. Then he had quailed at the thought of the explanations, the probing, the possibility of an investigation; more particularly, the problem of giving Hailey a legitimate voice and complaint.

Two more days, he reckoned, and then the whole deal would be tied up, and he would defy anyone to untangle the web of corporate intrigue that had brought the project to completion. Hailey could take a running jump at himself! It would take a bigger and better man than that outback farmer to bring down the complex structure that would soon begin to change the face of the countryside.

'Cheer up!' Mary was saying, breaking through his thoughts. 'Don't let that nasty episode upset you, dear.'

But she couldn't shake it from her memory. It was not only the horrible mess on the lawn; the man who had dumped it, Hailey, Stephen said it was, had seemed nearly demented as he tipped his truck and saw the load slip, faster and faster, on to the trimmed green square. Stephen said he was a crank; but she had seen tears in the man's eyes, and wondered.

He had been screaming something—'You can have them, Harcourt, they're not going to be any use to me!'—and when she had asked her husband what the man meant he had said the man was a maniac who wouldn't accept the inevitable. It had spoilt their day; a little devil of doubt had crept in, and Mary, whose belief in Stephen had always been complete, found it impossible to forget that furious, frustrated man, and wondered what such anguish could possibly have to do with this husband she knew so well— who had driven her to the park with a harsh, angry face that she barely recognised.

'But what...?' she had tried again, and he had turned on her.

'Leave it alone, Mary. You don't understand.'

'Then explain,' she had said with some asperity, and he had paused for a moment.

'Any development is likely to cut cross someone's interests,' he said at last. 'Hailey suffers from tunnel-vision. Now, let it go!'

So she did. But it took some time for the smoky air (an aroma she loved from childhood), the good companionship and the food and wine to bring her out of her dark and anxious mood. And, watching Stephen from a distance, she knew that it was not over for him, too.

The light burned late in Pirt's office that night, as Briggs and Verdun pored over the evidence. 'It's a gut feeling,' Verdun said. 'I don't know exactly why. But I think I know who.'

Briggs, let into the secret, raised his eyebrows. But before he could comment, the air was enriched by the fine singing voice of

Bingo Rafferty as he was assisted into the lock-up by Pirt. The two detectives went to the door.

'Need any help?' Nick Verdun asked.

Pirt was red in the face and clearly not pleased. 'Silly bugger can't hold his drink!' Bingo attempted to put his arms around the panting policeman's neck. 'Sit down, will you, you maniac?' Pirt roared, his patience running out.

Between them they secured Bingo, who was starting on *'O sole mio!'* for the fourth time, but never got past the first bars. (Unlike his meanderings during the evening just gone, presumably).

As they withdrew to the front of the station, Dulcet Merridew came into view, sitting on a hard bench, her feet neatly disposed underneath, her small person seemingly without a hair out of place.

'What are you doing here?' Verdun asked.

'I brought Bingo in,' she said, as if there was nothing the least bit strange about it.

Pirt, pulling his jacket down and slowly losing his ruddy complexion, said, 'You'd a' done him a favour if you'd let him rest where he was.'

'Oh, I don't think so,' she said reasonably. 'He was lying in the middle of the road. Someone might have run over him.'

'Very public-spirited of you,' Verdun commented, beginning to smile. He had grown to like Dulcet.

'I'm fond of Bingo.' She stood up, smoothing down her skirt and her hair, though neither needed it. 'He keeps asking me to marry him.'

'*Does* he?' Verdun said, grinning, and she smiled back, quite cheekily. 'And will you?'

'When I say *marry*, Mr Verdun, I am not quite accurate.' She picked up her handbag. 'He describes it as "the next best thing". I call it living in sin. I'm very old-fashioned.'

She made her way briskly towards the door. 'Well, gentleman! I must be off. Take care of Bingo,' she said to Pirt. 'He's rather a dear.'

Pirt watched her go. 'That woman's a nut-case,' he said lugubriously. 'And as for him...' Words failed him as he nodded towards the lock-up, where Bingo was now sleeping the sleep of intoxication. He yawned. 'You going to be long?'

Verdun turned off the office light. 'I think it'll wait until the morning,' he said, and strolled back with Briggs to the hotel.

Someone left a handbag with Pirt to give to 'that detective'. He handed it on to Briggs, who was awaiting Verdun's arrival in the office.

'Woman from the supermarket,' Pirt said laconically. 'Found it in the locker in the rest room, she says. Thinks it was Natalie Percy's.'

Briggs sat and looked at the bag. It wasn't the one she had had with her when he had been questioning her. That had been red—red plastic, a little worn, but with a big gilt buckle in good condition. This one was a bit tatty, the corners worn through, the colour faded. He would examine it before Verdun came in. It was Natalie's and he was still sensitive about her.

As it transpired, there was little enough in it. He put the objects out on the desk: a powder compact (not the one he had seen her use); a small packet of tissues that looked as if they had been there for a long time; a couple of wrapped lollies that had gathered fluff and gone sticky; and a notepad, spiral-topped, looking rather newer than anything else.

He leaned back and regarded them thoughtfully. What could the great detective learn from them?

Well…he was no expert on women's handbags, but this one seemed to lack certain basic things. No purse, no credit cards or any of the usual requirements of the kind. It looked, he decided, like a bag that had been taken out of a drawer somewhere and simply used for keeping something in. Hiding something in it, perhaps.

He picked up the compact and opened it, and that, too, looked old and unused. Only the notebook…

When Verdun came in, Briggs was waiting for him with a self-satisfied look on his face. 'What have you been up to?' the sergeant said. He himself was weary after another session with the luscious

Molly, who was, he strongly suspected, the vicar's candidate for the drug run.

Briggs gave him a quick run-down on the arrival of the bag.

'And?' said Verdun, loosening his tie.

'And—I think we've got proper confirmation about Natalie and Glencosset, sir.'

'Confirmation?' Verdun stopped to stare at his offsider. 'How do you mean?'

'Natalie wasn't as clever as the old woman at concealing meanings. It's all here. Obviously she hid the bag where it wouldn't be easily found, and...'

'Hang on a minute! What's this all about? Start from the beginning.'

When Briggs had brought him up to date Verdun nodded slowly. 'No wonder we can't find anything in her rooms. Who brought this in?'

'A Mrs Mabel Pollock. Works at the supermarket. She found it behind a locker when they were doing some renovations, thought she recognised it, saw Natalie's name under the flap—very wisely decided to bring it to us.'

'At last!' Verdun exclaimed. 'An intelligent woman!'

Briggs pulled a face. 'Well, not really, sir. I've had a talk to her, and intelligent isn't the word I'd have used.' He grinned. 'She asked if there'd be a reward!'

'So—show me.' Verdun sat down and held out his hand. Briggs passed the notebook to him. After a long silence, the sergeant sighed and put it down. 'Well, well, well! I was on the right track, anyway.'

'What do we do now, sir?'

'It's a pity she didn't bring it up to date. Those entries stop on the night Glencosset was killed. Look! *She called me into her dressing room—wants to see me on Sunday arvo. God, I wish she'd leave me alone.* We could have done with a final entry. Something like, *Meeting Mr X tonight*, and the date. Something we can show to the jury.' Verdun stood restlessly. 'There's an alarming lack of hard facts.'

27

Bingo Rafferty, eyes still unfocussed but brain slowly beginning to click into gear, went home that morning with no charges laid against him.

After he had left, Pirt found his few belongings in a plastic bag as they had been removed from his person, and tutted loudly at the lack of commonsense of his junior officers.

'Someone'll have to take this out to him,' he said; and Verdun, hearing him, at once thought it might pay dividends to get at Rafferty while he was, so to speak, on the wrong foot, and possibly more malleable than when fully sober.

So Nick Verdun and Briggs drove out to Bingo's disreputable block, and clambered over rusted metal and rotting wood until they located the master of chaos himself in the grateful shade of an ancient farm shed that leaned as drunkenly as its owner had done the night before.

'Can't leave a bloke alone, youse bastards,' he greeted them, without rancour. 'Goin' to turn my property upside-down again, are ya?'

Verdun sat down on an old oil drum, taking the chance that he'd ruin a good pair of strides. 'You blaming us for the mess, Mr Rafferty?'

'Who're you calling *Mr* Rafferty?' he demanded, peering at them through rose-tinted eyeballs. '*Bingo's* good enough for me friends.' The detective apologised.

Briggs was wandering about with the air of one enjoying a stroll in the park. Verdun held Bingo's gaze. 'We really do need to find Natalie's handbag,' he said mildly. 'It could be a very important clue—vital evidence.'

'If I had it,' Bingo assured him virtuously, 'I'd hand it to you quick-smart. But I haven't seen it.' He shielded his eyes against such sun as filtered into the shed. 'Dinkum, mate! You'd chuck a thing like that into the bush.'

'Ah, well,' Verdun sighed. 'You don't mind if we look?'

'Be my guest,' Rafferty said, popping the top of a tinny with practised ease. 'Go for your life, mate!'

Briggs found it. A gleam of red amongst a collection of soggy cartons full of rubbish caught his eye, and he risked tetanus and possibly the unfriendly interest of red-back spiders as he straddled a pile of old bumper bars and reached down to claim the missing handbag. Verdun, his face grim, advanced on Bingo Rafferty.

'Do you have an explanation?' he said in tones that demanded to be answered.

Bingo regarded the object with mild surprise. 'Never seen it before. Where was it?'

They led him to the spot. Briggs pointed. 'Did you put it there?'

Bingo, suddenly feeling that a little drop of what he fancied might well kill him, gave a long sigh and wiped his face with one calloused hand. 'No, mate. Never seen it. Someone's playing games with me.' He turned to peer at Verdun's dour expression. 'Straight up, guv—I never seen it.'

Nick stared at him for a long moment, then turned away slowly, looking around him at the squalid heaps of rubbish. He remembered the bag he had been holding, full of Bingo's own possessions. 'This is yours.' Bingo opened it to look inside. 'Don't leave town,' Verdun said at last. 'And get this—this midden cleared up!'

Bingo Rafferty watched the two men going towards the car. For a moment that passed all too soon he saw his empire through someone else's eyes and was ashamed. 'Here!' he whispered penetratingly to Briggs, 'what's a midden?'

Briggs, still holding the red handbag, didn't bother to answer. He was feeling very angry.

'It wasn't there when they searched,' Briggs said, breaking the silence. They had driven back to town and were sitting at Pirt's desk. 'No one could have missed it.'

'It's been planted,' Verdun agreed. 'Someone simply threw it into the muck and hoped it would either sink without trace or be linked with Rafferty.'

'*He* wouldn't throw it away, whatever he says. Bingo's a dealer. He'd have flogged it somewhere. Coupla bucks!'

'Yes.' Verdun frowned. 'Whoever it was probably didn't expect another search—not at Rafferty's, anyhow.' He picked up the bag. '*Was* it a plant? It's been wiped thoroughly. No fingerprints except ours. Nothing obvious seems to have been taken.' He opened it and spilt out the contents. 'What one would expect, I reckon. Purse with money, a bankcard—without which life today is unsupportable, God help us!—make-up, a spray-perfume bottle, a roll of peppermints, a handkerchief, a pen, a savings bank book, and so on and so on...'

He made a neat arrangement of them on the desk. 'No help at all, as far as I can see, Briggs. No hidden pockets, no secret diary, no lovers' notes or assignations, no *'Dear Madam, unless...'* letters—nothing!'

Briggs pulled the empty bag towards him and turned it in his hands. 'It was there with her,' he said tonelessly. 'When she was killed, this was there.' His lips were dry. 'Pity it can't speak, Sarge.'

Verdun was going through the contents as meticulously as if he hadn't done it twice already. He pulled the bank book out of its plastic cover and riffled the pages, revealing nothing but a savings total of two thousand one hundred dollars and forty-nine cents. He sighed, frustrated. 'It doesn't help, I'm afraid. Except that it was thrown away after we searched the first time. And that's no real help. Why not burn it? Chuck it in the bush? Did someone want to make trouble for Rafferty? The man makes enough trouble for himself.'

'What do we do now?'

Verdun leaned back and pondered. 'I think—I might ring Corinne again. Have another little chat.'

'What would she know?'

'I don't know exactly. Just a hunch. They were good friends, she and Natalie.'

'She's left town.'

'I've got a number.' He stood, suddenly energetic. 'I'll do it now.'

Briggs listened. Corinne was obviously being very reticent, but Verdun skilfully wore her down. His face was revealing, frustration giving way to conscious charm, then a sudden astonished raising of the eyebrows.

'Did she ring you that evening? She did. My dear girl, why didn't you tell me?... Of course, *everything* matters in a case like this...She said that? That she was going to meet him?... Oh, *them*! Are you sure?... Well, he would say that, wouldn't he, to cover himself? She wouldn't have gone if he'd been alone...No, I'm sure you didn't see—that's why you didn't suspect...but I do. And thank you, Corinne. Thank you very much. Better late than never... Goodbye...yes, all right, goodbye!'

He stared at Briggs. 'She didn't think it could be them, not both of them, *so she didn't mention it!* Can you believe it, Briggs? Didn't want to cause any more trouble! Because of who it was, she didn't mention...' He stopped, bemused. 'What do they think we're doing here? Making up fairy tales?'

But all at once a look of pure relief spread across his face. 'But we've got him, Briggs—we've got him!' He pushed his chair back and stretched his legs. He felt as if he had run a mile, weary yet exultant. 'We'll bring him in for questioning. With this information we have something to throw at him that he'll find very hard to refute.' He leaned back. 'We might go and see Simon Lee as well,' he said thoughtfully. 'This is going to create quite a stir. Someone will have to be prepared to pick up the pieces.'

Briggs said, 'Are you going to tell me?'

'In the car,' he said, putting his hand on the young man's shoulder. 'But first, back to the school. One more search.'

'What a pity,' said the constable flatly, trying to avoid emotion, 'that Natalie didn't come to us.'

'She'd learnt the lesson of deviousness. She'd had a first-rate teacher.'

Mrs Parker let Nick Verdun and Briggs into the headmistress's study, then tactfully left them alone. 'I shall be glad to see the back of this place,' Verdun said. 'It's getting me down.'

'Looks OK to me,' Briggs said, wandering round the walls where there were good prints and original oils that Verdun had never had time to look at properly.

'Looks fine,' Verdun agreed. 'That's the problem. The woman was obviously potty, but the room looks incredibly respectable and normal. There's not sign anywhere of her being off-balance except in those wretched diaries.' He was searching along the row to those earlier volumes of the Glencosset saga that he had never bothered to look at, because he had not considered the fact that her death might have been caused by events that had taken place before she came to the school.

A pile of leather-bound books, clearly much older than the ones he had been immersed in for so many days, lay on the bottom shelf of all, almost out of sight. He lifted them up, out on to the desk, and read the dates on the fading spines.

'How long ago would she have been in college?' he asked Briggs, who had no idea. 'Well, she was fifty-one. So we can assume that the volume I'm after would be about thirty years ago, give or take.'

'Mediaeval history!' Briggs said, for whom thirty years of life were still a considerable way ahead.

Verdun groaned a little. 'Why would anyone want to document her life to such an extent? What was she going to do with all this accumulated knowledge?'

'Write her memoirs? My grandma kept diaries all her life.'

'And did she write her memoirs?'

'No. She gave them to my father and he lost them when they had a house fire after she died.'

'Sad!' said Verdun, not without a tinge of sarcasm. 'Your family seems to have pursued me throughout this case, Briggs. Are there many more?'

'Yes, sir. A very prolific family, on both sides. My young sister...'

'Spare me, Briggs.'

'I just thought you'd be interested to know that she's joining the force next year.' Verdun's face said enough. 'Sorry, Sarge!' Briggs grinned widely.

'Ah!' Verdun said suddenly. 'I think we've got it!' He stood up, book in hand, opened in the middle. 'This one has been used quite a lot, and quite recently, too. It opened at the place. Listen—this is a Friday. *"New student Jasper Spenlow came today. Handsome in a rather obvious way. But charming!"* Then, a week later. *"JS asked me to go to the theatre with him. Shaw. Would have preferred Shaks: but at least I'm going to get to know HIM better!"* Quite girlish, young Teresa, in those days.'

He turned pages, came to the next entry. *"JS and I went on the river together. Heaven! So sophisticated. Such jealousy among girls! Delightful."* She liked being the leader even then. Here's another. *"JS said no time to waste this weekend. Didn't know what we were doing was wasting time! He must get his priorities in order."* That's our Teresa, eh? *"JS quite unreasonable. Says for my good but he's lying. MK saw him with Patricia. He'd better watch out!"* What have we got? A bad case of jealousy?'

'How could anything that happened back then be the basis of a murder today?' Briggs considered the idea. 'Though I suppose if it was jealousy a lifetime ago, and if they lived in the same little town for more than ten years...'

'*And* he taught music in her school!'

'Yes...' Briggs was frowning. 'But what could possibly bring something like that to a head? Surely she wasn't trying to get him back again?'

'She was obsessive, clearly. Ah-ha—here's something else. "*So it is Patricia! He told me that what we had was something special—has he been saying the same things to her? If so, he can watch out.*" Always threats, A very possessive person. Not a happy woman. Everything points to it.'

'So what was in her mind? Retribution?'

'Oh-oh—here's where the plot thickens. "*MK told me today...I can hardly write the words. Patricia told her (in confidence), but of course MK would tell me. She knows what I will do if she doesn't.*" She's even got her knife into MK. "*Patricia is pregnant!!! And JS is frantic about it. Serves him right—and her! Particularly her. I would kill her if I could get away with it. I hope her baby will be blind and deaf and deformed... How dare she?*"'

'Oh dear,' Verdun said, putting the book down on the desk. 'You can't help wondering what Miss Glencosset's background was. Such venom!'

'OK, said Briggs. 'So the boy-friend had got another girl into trouble, and Miss G would like to kill her. What's that got to do with what happened here?'

Verdun gazed across the room. 'You really wouldn't wait thirty years or so to get back at him, would you? Do you think any girl would do that?'

'I wouldn't know. I'm not a girl, and that was another world. The permissive society wasn't even a word.'

Verdun was reading on. Suddenly he sat up. 'My God! It's here. Listen... "*JS came to see me tonight. How could he! He was disgusting, in tears, slobbering all over me. Because of HER! She can't do anything right, stupid fool. Insists on having the baby, then says her parents'll kill her. He should save them the trouble.*" Then this, three days later: "*Terrific fuss all over coll. because of Patricia. Everyone thinks it was an accident, but I know better. That spineless idiot finally*" *did something about it. I made him write it down. It could come in useful.'"*

Verdun looked at Briggs, his eyes hard. 'What? What happened to Patricia?'

'Killed her, Sarge?' They stared at each other. 'Is that what it's all been about? He killed the girl, and Miss G held it over him all these years?' He sat forward eagerly. 'Did she come here because she knew he was here? It would have been perfect—if she'd wanted to keep him on the hop.'

'That paper—the one she said he had written? A woman who kept all these diaries wouldn't have lost the all-important confession.'

He riffled the diary's pages, then opened the ends and shook it. Neatly held at the very back of the book was a thin piece of paper in a plastic covering. Verdun drew it out and spread it on the desk.

The writing was a little faded, and the paper had yellowed around the edges. But the message was still very clear. *'I, Jasper Spenlow, confess that I killed Patricia West on Thursday, May 12, by hitting her over the head and then pushing her off the college tower just after sunset. I did this because she was having my baby, and it would have created an impossible situation for both of us."*

The two detectives sat silent, looking down at the confession, drawn out of a supremely selfish young man by an egocentric young woman when he was at her mercy. 'They were well suited,' Verdun said at last. 'This was more than a confession of murder. It was an *invitation* to murder! What must he have thought when she turned up here at the school? How often did he decide to finish it?'

'So why on that particular day? Why did she ring him? Had she done it often? Was this the last straw? And why ring the others?'

'I don't know,' Verdun admitted. 'Unless she was cracking up. Her recent diaries indicate that she thoroughly enjoyed the distress she could cause. The girls here were scared of her.' He stopped. 'The day of the dress rehearsal—on the face of it, it makes no sense. Why upset everybody on that day of all days?'

'Perhaps she liked the sense of impending doom—just knowing that all eyes were on her, not only because she was Katisha, but because she had them in her power. What a mess!' Briggs stretched his arms above his head and yawned. 'What now?'

'Time to move,' Verdun said slowly. 'You know, something more *must* have occurred that day to precipitate what happened. What? Everything else points to the fact that she was simply jiggling everybody up a bit—almost as if it was fun for her. So there's something else, and we don't know what.' He collected all the papers together, put the 'confession' into an envelope, and replaced the diaries on the shelf, keeping out only the one with the damning evidence in it.

'Where to?'

'The bit I don't like,' Verdun said. 'We'll go and see Simon Lee, and then pull Spenlow in. We've got enough against him, with this evidence, to justify an arrest. The Patricia thing, for starters.'

'Poor Natalie,' Briggs said, not for the first time. 'Getting mixed up in that old spider's web. She didn't have a chance.'

'Let it be a lesson to you, young Briggs.' His mouth curved grimly, and there was no smile in his eyes.

28

'What clinched it,' said Verdun, 'was the diaries. I had my suspicions, but in the end it was the need of both dead women to put things down on paper that helped solve their murders.'

Simon Lee waited patiently. He was not sure he wanted to hear what conclusions the detective had come to.

'Miss Glencosset had a veritable library of diaries going back to the year dot. Natalie Percy had a notepad on which, among other things, she had kept details of her uneasy relationship with her ex-headmistress.'

'What was that relationship?' Lee asked.

'She had fallen into Glencosset's hands while she was still at school.' He related the sad tale, Simon Lee tutting now and then. 'She was in an invidious position. As long as Miss Glencosset was there, Natalie feared for her child's happiness. Without Miss Glencosset, Natalie would never know where the child was. Either way she was the loser. So she picked up odd bits of gossip, as ordered, and relayed them back, going at night when no one wold see her. Miss Glencosset stored them and used them to build dossiers on those she hated. Hatred,' he said sombrely, 'played a big part in the lady's life.'

'But Natalie could never have been a source for anything of importance, surely? That kind of local gossip isn't a reason for murder, is it?'

'Miss G, by virtue of her position in the town, was also able to collect the little pieces of information which, gradually assembled, created damning pictures of some of the local power-brokers. And a number of *them*,' he commented without giving anything away, 'will spend their day in court as a result. Someone else will take care of them. Fortunately, I'm not required to uncover every little detail—only the two big, squalid murders!' He made a grimace. 'She was a menace, all right. Though in this case perhaps she had her uses.'

'So you were able to see a pattern in these writings?'

'Yes—but I didn't really think they added up to homicide. That seemed to need something more soul-searing. And I was stumped until someone unwittingly handed me the clues.'

Simon Lee regarded the detective steadily. 'Who are we talking about, Sergeant Verdun.? Who killed these women?'

Verdun met his gaze. 'Jasper Spenlow! Mrs Spenlow told me something at the barbecue, thinking that I already knew it. She told me that Miss G and her husband had been college students together.'

Simon's eyes opened wide. 'Indeed! So—was there something in the past that could have led to this tragedy?'

'There was.' Verdun told him of the brief romance, Jasper's infidelity, and finally the murderous act that had hung over him from youth to middle-age. Simon felt revulsion rising in him.

'But Maggie knew nothing of that!'

'No—I'm sure she didn't.'

'Maggie is a tough, occasionally even an unpleasant woman. But she would have no part in such a cover-up.'

'So, while Miss Glencosset appeared to be a good friend to Spenlow—he taught at her school, she performed in his operas—she was making him eat the dust of humiliation. She had his confession, in his own hand, and I'm sure she didn't let him forget it.'

'What brought it all to the boil?'

'I don't know. I hope he'll tell me. Spenlow has always said she didn't ring him that afternoon. But she had a real campaign of vengeance on the phone that day, and I think when he is faced with it he may well admit that she had stepped up her demands in some way. Certainly she had caused consternation among locals who had good cause to resent her—as you yourself know.'

Lee frowned. 'But you can't really be sure, Sergeant, can you?'

'Not without Natalie's evidence. And then Corinne's.' He told Lee about the recent phone call. 'Natalie and Briggs had been seen by Spenlow, talking in the park. As she walked home he caught up with her in the arcade. He seems to have been quite charming at first, but then he got nasty about what she had been telling the police.

'He was so strange, so she told Corinne, that she refused to say anything, and he grabbed her arm and threatened to tell everybody that she was a constant visitor to Miss Glencosset. She defied him. Said what did he mean, how did he know, and what did it matter anyway? When he said that people would think she was 'gay', that made her mad. She said she'd tell everybody that she'd seen him go back into the Green Room when he said he'd been outside, waiting for Maggie. The way she put it to Corinne was that 'that'll cook his goose even if it's not true. Let him wriggle out of that!'

Lee shook his head slowly. 'I suppose that neither of the girls could really believe that someone they knew so well, and for so long, could be a murderer.'

'It's always hard to believe.'

'So that was, in a way, the catalyst?'

'According to Corinne, he went white in the face and glared at Natalie. She thought he was going to hit her. But he said he was sorry, he'd not been feeling well, and Maggie had been saying would Natalie like to drop in for coffee sometime—there was a new drama they wanted her to read for. But Natalie was a bit put off. So he tried again. Said why not go to the theatre later on, and he and Maggie would meet her there at eight?'

Lee tutted gently, his eyes dark with sadness.

'Corinne was sure she wouldn't have gone if it had been just Spenlow—not in a fit, she said. But Maggie was a different matter. She liked Maggie. So she said yes.' Verdun stopped. So pathetic, he was thinking. So innocent. 'But thank God she rang Corinne.'

Simon Lee was silent as he finished. 'Poor child,' he murmured at last. 'So she died for a piece of tit-for-tat, not realising that it was true.' He shook his head slowly. 'And Maggie, I assume, knew nothing of all this? Jasper... Well—I'm not altogether surprised. He's a man of many moods.' He raised his eyes to Verdun's. 'What now, Sergeant?'

'The part I don't like. I'm on my way to arrest Jasper Spenlow. I didn't want to do so without first making sure that there was someone ready to hold the fort when the news breaks.' A self-conscious flicker touched his face briefly. 'I've grown quite fond of this little community.'

Simon Lee inclined his head gravely, his face pale, taut with shock. 'I wish we had met in less traumatic times.'

Nick Verdun rose and held out his hand. In a matter of minutes he would be ringing the Spenlow's door bell, and he wanted to get it over and done with.

As he slid into the car beside Briggs he could see Simon waving gently against the back-lighting from his hallway.

'Nice old bloke,' Briggs said. 'Spenlow's place?'

Verdun nodded. 'Let's finish it, sunshine!'

29

'I've been offered a job,' Jasper said. 'In Hong Kong.'

'Hong Kong?' Maggie looked up, a quick frown crossing her face. 'I don't think I fancy that much. What is it?'

'Music department. They want me to expand it.'

'Hong Kong isn't what it was. With China…'

'I don't care.' He stared at her across the table, seeing her properly for the first time in a decade: the sharp-chinned face he had once thought 'elfin', the quick flow of impatient expressions he had seen as the inner glow of character, the long-legged nervous energy that had seemed to him, in their courting days, as attractive as an unbroken filly awaiting a master. Had he really thought he could break her in, put a bridle on her, harness that liveliness for his own delectation? If so, he had been wrong! He knew that she despised him—and all at once it didn't matter. 'I'll take my chance.'

'Well, I'm not sure I will.' She glanced up at him again, and once he would have taken the warning, backed down, shut up.

'That's not important,' he said, quite calm now the decision had been made.

'Not important? What do you mean?'

What did he mean? How should he dress it up, this coming to terms with everything that was wrong between them? He took a deep breath. The truth, unvarnished, unconcealed! Perhaps he owed her that, at least.

'I'm going on my own. By myself.'

Maggie lowered the paper. He had her attention now, all right.

'By yourself?' He nodded, watching her face. The sudden frown came again, making her look older, drawn, not at all elfin. 'What do you mean—by yourself?'

'Without you.'

The frown became calculating, the eyes gleamed icily. 'With someone else?'

'No.'

'*On your own?*' She was angry now. He wondered why. 'Not even with someone else? You're leaving me—for no good reason?'

He stood, folding his napkin carefully, brushing a crumb from his shirt-front. 'For the best reason,' he said, as kindly as he could. 'Because we have nothing for each other anymore. I want to be able to live again, to breathe again…!'

Her head went back suddenly and she laughed, a harsh, crowing sound that shattered any finer feelings he might have retained.

'You…?' she said, gasping in her paroxysm. 'You? *To live and breathe again*…! Oh God! How trite, how pathetic!'

Jasper left the table. He knew that laugh would go with him, to Hong Kong, to wherever he might venture anywhere in the world, corroding all he did, destroying every good relationship, poisoning any atmosphere in which he might search for peace, for tranquillity. He thought of Teresa Glencosset, of that moment when he had told her that the game was over, that he was leaving, freeing himself from her clutches. He heard again the cold, triumphant voice, could imagine the twist of the lips; he recalled without emotion his understanding that there was only one way out for him.

The abundant life had been taken in a few moments of time, the essence of what she had once been reduced eventually to an urnful of ashes. He remembered Natalie, brimming with life and then suddenly lifeless. And, briefly, he half-remembered a girl called Patricia.

Maggie watched him with coldly amused eyes, eyes that he had once adored, and the laughter seemed to swell and roar around him like a torrent, sweeping him towards destruction, drowning the sound of the front door bell.

'What a fool you are!' she cried at last, and he made his final decision.

Before he left for Hong Kong— somehow, *she* would have to die, too.

Impatiently, Nick Verdun banged on the door.

'Still seems odd, after so long,' Briggs said as they took the road north to the city. 'Spenlow's sudden decision to kill Glencosset.'

'Because he'd decided to cut loose. Must have thought Hong Kong was well outside her range. He'd decided to take this teaching job there, leaving Maggie behind. I *thought* those two were at breaking point. He faced Glencosset with it during the notorious phone call. And she retaliated by saying she'd tell everyone about that girl at college, all those years ago. Silly threat, really. If she'd known about it that long she was virtually an accessory after the fact. But such niceties probably passed her by—she was totally ego-centred, thought nothing could touch her. Spenlow presumably exploded, and decided to do away with her.'

'But Natalie…'

'Yes, Natalie.' Verdun sighed. 'When Natalie rang to "tell all", including the hoax drama reading, and then was killed, Corinne must surely have expected Jasper to come looking for her, too. Though perhaps not. There's still a lot of innocence about out there…' He made an exasperated sound. 'Couldn't she see her only real safety was if *we* knew?'

Briggs was silent as he drove. A flock of black cockatoos crossed the road, squawking as if in pain. The sun was sinking behind the trees.

'And the others, Sarge? Parkinson and Harcourt and all—what will you do about them?'

'Pirt's job! I've left him a *little list*.' He grinned drily. 'Parkinson's OK, because no one's pressing charges. But Harcourt! A nasty bit of work, I reckon. His land deal is probably illegal—or nearly so. Not my bag! They'll send someone from Fraud to sort it out.'

Briggs grinned back. 'What about Bingo? You should be able to get him on *something*!'

'Bingo! I should think the health authorities should have a sniff at his cess-pit. I don't know how he can live in it.'

They fell silent, each with personal memories of the little town they were leaving behind. 'Molly de Vance,' said Briggs. 'The reverend was right about her.'

'I'm afraid so. She's booked for Singapore. They'll let her go, pick her up when she comes back. Customs job. If the Singapore police don't get her.' Verdun gave a brief laugh. 'And her would-be boyfriend, the butcher, has a little problem with illegal carcases. I don't know what they do to farmers who sell outside the regulations.' He yawned widely. 'Silly bugger! He'd got a nice little business there.'

'What a mess.' Briggs tried not to catch the yawn from his superior, but failed.

'You can say that again.'

'Do you think,' the constable said after a while, 'that Spenlow had this in mind when he asked Mrs Parkinson to understudy Katisha?'

'It's a thought,' Verdun said.

A few kilometres nearer to their destination, Briggs said, 'I was a bit surprised he gave in so quickly. I thought we might have a bit of a struggle.'

'It's odd,' Verdun said. 'I've seen great hulking brutes of murderers behave like pussy cats when they're arrested, and the mildest little men who look as if they can't say 'boo!' suddenly becoming raging maniacs. You never know how it's going to take them.' He thought back over the few hours now safely behind them; Spenlow had opened the door to them, and stood back to let them in. Without knowing why, Verdun had felt that any fight there had been in the man had somehow dissipated; and when he looked at Maggie he could perhaps see the reason. She seemed to be suffering from an ice-cold fury; when they entered the room, Jasper behind them, she looked at the two detectives with freezing disdain.

'What now?' she said.

Verdun turned to her husband. In his most official voice he said, 'Mr Spenlow, evidence has come to hand which now convinces me that you can answer my questions with rather more honesty than you have done so far.'

Jasper sighed. 'Why don't you sit down?' He indicated a chair by the dining table. Verdun ignored the invitation. Maggie, standing impatiently, glared at the three men facing her.

'What is it you want, Sergeant? Haven't we been bothered enough?'

'Mrs Spenlow, you may want to have someone with you. Is there anyone you want to call?'

She stared at him; and a sudden flicker in the eyes indicated that something of what was to come had dawned on her. She turned to look at her husband, who was avoiding her gaze. 'Jasper...?'

'Let him say what he's come to say,' Jasper said, voice flat. He moved slowly to the window and looked out into the garden.

'Miss Glencosset kept many diaries,' Verdun said. 'And according to her entries she had her fingers in many local pies. Among them, your name crops up several times with enough information to make you a leading suspect in the crimes that have been committed in this town recently.'

'Teresa Glencosset,' Jasper said in a weary voice, 'was an interfering old bitch.'

'So we assumed from her diaries. Now, I would like you to tell me what happened on the evening she was killed.'

Maggie's eyes were flashing from one man to the other. 'What are you talking about, Sergeant? Jasper's *told* you, several times.'

'But not the truth, Mrs Spenlow. Have you, sir?'

'Why don't you shut up, Maggie?' Jasper turned from the window. His wife's mouth fell open. 'Let's get this over.' He went to the table and pulled out a chair. 'All right if I sit down?' he said, without any trace of irony in his voice. 'I feel rather tired.'

Verdun regarded him for a moment. The man looked exhausted. 'Jasper Spenlow,' he said in a voice devoid of emotion, 'I am arresting you for the murders of Teresa Glencosset and Natalie Percy...' Jasper nodded slowly.

Maggie sank into her chair. 'What possible evidence could you have against Jasper? Look at him—a *murderer?* Ridiculous! He hasn't got the guts...'

Jasper gave a brief, strangely peaceful smile. 'Get used to it, Maggie. You haven't looked at me for years. I'm not the person you always tell me I am.' He looked up at Verdun. 'I suppose you really do have the evidence?'

'I am also arresting you for the murder of Patricia West.' He completed the required rigmarole and turned to the constable. 'Cuffs, Briggs.'

Jasper's face showed momentary shock, then cleared. 'Yes, of course! Patricia. That was a pity.' He regarded the handcuffs Briggs produced with what almost seemed like interest. 'What now?'

'I wonder what will happen to Maggie,' Briggs said as they drove onward into the night. 'Her balloon was properly pricked, wasn't it? You could almost see her wondering how the G and S would take the news. Perhaps she's more sensitive than she looks.'

A faint snore answered him. He glanced around and grinned, and they swept on in silence. The way home seemed long; but Verdun, suddenly tired beyond belief, slept away some of the tensions unavoidable in a homicide case.

After a while, discreetly under his breath, Briggs began to hum a tune. It was sometime before he located the words that fitted it, and when he did he wondered what kind of subconscious interlinking had produced that particular memory out of his recent past.

'*Everything is a source of fun,*' he sang under his breath. '*Nobody's safe, for we care for none! Life is a joke that's just begun! Three little maids from school!*' He would remember this case—and Natalie.

Simon Lee walked in his garden and felt the benison of the sinking sun, and the perfumes of cut grass and flowers.

There was justice, he was thinking; after all this time, there was justice. 'The mills of God,' he murmured as he brushed past lavender and bent to touch the bright head of a daisy. For the first time in many, many years there were the faint sensations of true tranquillity in his tormented breast.

Strange that Glencosset had never picked up this particular agony and exploited it. Thank God for that, and for the fact that therefore he had not had to reveal it to the detective. With Jasper Spenlow gone, hopefully for good, he would say goodbye to the grieving past. He would be able to face his own weakness and failures, sort out his life. Perhaps it would even be possible to forgive himself, to let judicial vengeance take the place of the punishment he had always known he should have meted out, for Katie's sake, for Lois's, for his own.

Inside the house he stood for a while before the photograph of his daughter as she laughed up into the camera, her mother smiling beside her: a happy family memento, taken less than a year before everything had turned to dust and ashes.

He moved slowly, exhausted with emotion, and stood by the window to watch the sun as it slipped away. 'Katie!' he whispered. 'Katie!' Losing her had been somehow even worse than seeing Lois turn from him in cold anger. Perhaps he would have done something about Spenlow if he had not been embattled by her bitterness—but perhaps he had simply used that bitterness as an excuse for his own lack of strength, of dynamism. Whatever the reason, he had borne the guilt for all the years of heartbreak, and despised himself.

What did a word mean? Seduction? A small word to have the power to destroy a whole family. Spenlow had seduced little Katie, just past her fifteenth birthday—that was bad, it was evil to take a child and destroy purity, innocence. But worse was the destruction of trust; Katie's wide eyes, in love with life, had narrowed, grown old; and by the time Lois had told him the reason for the change in his daughter it was too late. His quiet affection had not been adequate for the challenge.

If he had had the courage, he now asked himself, would he have killed Spenlow and so saved Teresa Glencosset and Natalie? For Natalie's sake, he wished he could have done so. For Miss Glencosset's…? That was a thought he could not yet face.

With the rich warmth of the sun caressing him through the window, he wondered why he had stayed here in this town. Why hadn't he gone, followed Lois, lived anywhere else but within sight and sound of Jasper Spenlow? Why allow the constant friction of contact with the man? At least he had an answer to that one. Somewhere, far down inside himself, he acknowledged that he had wanted to keep his enemy under his eye (knowing what he knew: knowing that Spenlow didn't know he knew it), turn the knife in his own wounds, wait—for what? Well, possibly for this moment, when at last the man would be brought crashing down.

'But not by me,' Simon said to the sun; 'not by me! I lacked the strength. And I must live with that.'

His eyes were full of tears; and the last sunbeams blinded him with rainbows.

In the cool shadows of St Edmund's church, the Rev Charles Culbert was kneeling at the altar rail. He had intended to pray, but could find no words. Tomorrow he would conduct Natalie Percy's funeral, and he had written to the bishop asking for a few days off afterwards, during which he could try to get himself together.

When he left the church to walk slowly home he recalled that there was no bread in the house, and he turned his steps towards the supermarket. It was on his mind that he ought to go and see Maggie Spenlow, to commiserate, to ask if there was anything he could do. But he acknowledged his own futility. He couldn't think what he would say to her.

'Well,' said a voice as he stowed his loaf into a plastic bag, 'we meet again!' His heart did a double shuffle in his chest. He didn't need to look to know it was Molly.

His feet wanted to run, but with a sudden stiffening of moral fibre he turned slowly and looked down at the diminutive, provocative figure.

'Get thee behind me, Satan!' he said, quite gently, and left, walking with his head up, his heart suddenly at peace.

THE END

BIOGRAPHY

BARBARA YATES ROTHWELL lived, married and brought up six children in Surrey, England, before emigrating to Western Australia in 1974 with her musician husband and their two youngest daughters. Her other children arrived in Australia in due course.

Also a musician and a trained singer, she was for 10 years in the 1980s a music reviewer for The West Australian newspaper. In the UK she had been Women's Page Editor for a large group of weekly papers.

After founding and running Yanchep Community School in Western Australia for 8 years, and having successfully written and sold short stories in several countries, Barbara decided it was time to break out into novel writing. Her teenage historical novel, THE BOY FROM THE HULKS, was published in 1994 by Longman Cheshire, and in 1998 her historical novel largely based on the Yanchep area, DUTCH POINT, was published privately in the UK.

Since then she has been publishing with Trafford in Canada/ America, a Print on Demand company that gives her full control of her books. This has been a very satisfactory development. She has now brought out 11 books with Trafford, and there are more ideas in the pipeline.

Barbara has also written plays, of which two full-length and some one-act comedies have been performed by community theatres in Wanneroo, Perth and Coonabarabran, NSW, and one short play for a young cast in Bunbury, which won a commendation.

Some of her books can be found on her website: www. barbarayatesrothwell.com and they are available from internet book stores. She can be reached at the contact page.

BOOKS BY BARBARA YATES ROTHWELL

The Boy from the Hulks...1st edition

Dutch Point...historical saga

Coulter Valley...family mystery

Klara...fiction based on fact,
the personal story of a Jewish refugee

Ripple in the Reeds...a French girl
marries a Nazi in pre-war Europe

No time for pity...short story collection

Standfast...short story collection

An Empty Bottle...third short story collection

A Fragment of Life...autobiography in
her legal name, Hebe Morgan.
Written by her alter ego, Barbara.

The Boy from the Hulks...2nd edition with sequel

Death at the Festival...a murder-mystery

Through a brick wall, darkly...a story of adoption

Contact through *barbarayatesrothwell.com*